#2
HOME RUN HERO

DEAN HUGHES

ALADDIN PAPERBACKS

First Aladdin Paperbacks edition March 1999

Aladdin Paperbacks
An imprint of Simon & Schuster
Children's Publishing Division
1230 Avenue of the Americas
New York, NY 10020

Also available in an Atheneum Books for Young Readers hardcover edition.

Designed by Amanda Foley

The text for this book was set in Caslon 540 Roman.

Printed and bound in the United States of America

10   9   8   7   6   5   4   3   2   1

The Library of Congress has cataloged the hardcover edition as follows:
Hughes, Dean, 1943–
Home run hero / by Dean Hughes.
p.   cm. — (Scrappers ; #2)
Summary: The players on his summer league baseball team, the Scrappers, have some talent, but Wilson is discouraged because they have an attitude problem and trouble working together as a team.
ISBN 0-689-81925-0 (hc)
[1. Baseball—Fiction. 2. Teamwork (Sports)—Fiction.] I. Series: Hughes, Dean, 1943–   Scrappers ; #2.
PZ7.H87312Hi   1999
[Fic]—dc21   98-10874
ISBN 0-689-81934-X (pbk)

CHAPTER ONE

Wilson Love adjusted his catcher's mask. It was a hot evening, and sweat was running down his face. But he didn't worry about that. He was trying to decide what to do with this next batter.

It was the top of the third inning, with two outs and a runner on third. The batter, a guy named Kevin, hit ninth in the Hot Rods' lineup. He was small, so Wilson assumed he wasn't much at bat. Still, the kid was mouthy, and he was wearing wraparound shades like he was some kind of all-star. Maybe he was *all* mouth, and maybe he wasn't.

A lot of the Hot Rods were wearing the mirrored sunglasses, but Wilson had heard that they dressed a lot better than they played. They were sponsored by a local automotive performance shop, and they looked it: gleaming red and white uniforms with silver trim, like race car drivers. Wilson figured those uniforms must have cost five times as much as the Scrappers'.

Kevin dug his spikes in like he was ready to swing for the fence. *This kid thinks he's Barry Bonds*, Wilson thought. *He's gonna swing at anything.* So Wilson signaled a fastball to his pitcher, Adam Pfitzer, and set the target low and away.

Adam nodded, wound up, and fired hard. The ball was outside, but Kevin took a wild swing and missed.

Wilson tossed the ball back to Adam as the infield players talked it up. Gloria Gibbs, the Scrappers' shortstop, was shouting the loudest. "Good heat, Adam."

Adam's confidence was growing. He'd gotten lit up in the first inning for four hits and two runs. With a runner on third now, and his team down 2 to 0, Wilson didn't want the ninth batter to get lucky and put them in a deeper hole.

Adam's next pitch was straight down the barrel. The ball popped into Wilson's mitt, and Kevin never moved. Strike two.

The guys on the Hot Rods' bench really worked Kevin over. "What are you waiting for? *That* was your pitch!" they were yelling.

All the Scrappers were talking it up, but Adam hardly seemed to notice. He had a way of disappearing into his own world. He usually pitched best when his eyes looked a little glassy.

Again, Wilson signaled for a low fastball. No reason to try any breaking stuff against this batter, especially when the hard stuff was working. Wilson had the feeling Kevin was going to swing at anything close this time. Adam smiled just a little and nodded. He knew it, too.

The pitch had some real smoke on it, but it was way low. It didn't matter, though. Kevin swung so wildly he almost fell down. Strike three.

Wilson laughed, tossed the ball to the ump, and ran to the dugout. Adam loped off the mound and got to Wilson just as he was peeling off his shin guards. "Hey, great calls. We really got into that guy's head."

"You've got your fastball smoking," Wilson told him. "We're going to get these guys now."

Wilson actually believed that, too. But he knew that Adam could do well for a while and then fall apart. In fact, the whole team was that way. The Scrappers had some good talent, but everyone had a lot to learn.

Wilson was on deck, so he grabbed a bat. He took a couple of warm-up swings as he watched his friend Robbie Marquez slam a hard grounder past the third baseman. Robbie ran hard to first and made the turn, but Wanda Coates, the assistant coach, held up her hands and shouted, "Hold up!"

As Wilson headed to the plate, Adam yelled, "Okay, Wilson, jack one over the fence. Let's get those runs back."

All the Scrappers picked up the chant. "*Lose* one, Wilson. Put it in the parking lot."

The Hot Rods' pitcher, a big muscular kid named Jake Oates, took his hat off and wiped his face with his sleeve. But the guy wasn't sweating because of Wilson. Wilson had struck out in the first inning on just four pitches.

This was only the third game of the season, but everyone knew what Wilson could do. He could whack the ball out of sight when he connected. But he struck out a lot, too. And that was something Wilson wanted to change. He knew he could be more consistent.

The first pitch came in fast and outside. Wilson took a savage swing at it and got nothing but air. His teammates stopped yelling.

Wilson was embarrassed, but he took his stance again and got himself ready for the next pitch. Everyone made fun of the way he bent so far forward and held his bat so high, but it was the stance that felt natural to him.

Oates shook off the first sign, which made Wilson suspicious. Then when he threw, the pitch was high, a little inside, and spinning. Wilson had seen that before. *Curveball*, he told himself, and he held back. As the pitch broke over the plate, he took a fierce cut.

The bat rang in his hands, and Wilson knew, instantly, that the ball was gone. It took off on a beautiful arc. The left fielder only took a few steps back before he stopped and watched the ball drop far beyond the fence. Home run.

Wilson couldn't help but grin as he rounded the bases. His teammates all ran out from the dugout and greeted him with high fives. "You're the man," his friend Robbie shouted, and that felt good.

"Let's keep it going," Wilson shouted to the rest of the players. He didn't know how it had happened, but he felt like the star of this team. Robbie and Gloria and Thurlow were all better players, but they weren't driving in runs the way Wilson was.

The Scrappers got a couple more hits that inning, but they couldn't bring them home. Adam was still in command, though. When he faced the top of the lineup, he got the Hot Rods out, one-two-three.

Leading off in the bottom of the fourth, Tracy Matlock came up with the score still tied 2 to 2. She always looked good in practice—a solid line-drive hitter. But for some reason she had gotten only a couple of singles in the games. Wilson knew the Scrappers needed to score more runs, and it was frustrating to know that the team's best offensive weapon—Thurlow Coates—was sitting next to him on the bench.

Thurlow was a tall, strong kid, far and away the best athlete on the team. But he had yet to start a game for the Scrappers. He didn't even play much.

Thurlow usually showed up late to practice,

and then he didn't put out any real effort. He claimed it was because he didn't like baseball, but Wilson knew that wasn't true. All this bad attitude stuff was new, and it seemed to be directed at his mother, who had volunteered to be the assistant coach. Wilson knew what Coach Carlton was thinking. He wouldn't start Thurlow until the guy showed that he wanted to play.

At the plate, Tracy seemed hesitant to swing, but her patience paid off. She worked Oates for a walk.

Wilson clapped and shouted, "Okay, Martin, bring her in." But he didn't believe for a minute that would happen. Martin Epting was not much of a hitter.

"I wish we had you out there," Wilson told Thurlow.

Thurlow didn't respond for a moment, as though he might be thinking the same thing. But then he said, "Naw. I like it this way. I don't have to shower after the games."

Wilson had played sports with Thurlow before, and he knew the guy was a power hitter. "Come on, Thurlow, you know you'd rather be playing. You just don't want to give in to your mom."

"I wouldn't mind playing on a good team. But these guys are a bunch of losers."

Wilson looked down the bench. Luckily, no one seemed to have heard Thurlow. They were watching as Martin stood like a statue and let strike three go by.

Wilson tried not to sound mad, but he said, "Thurlow, what's going on? You never used to be like this. You're going to waste your whole summer on the bench just so you can win some lame argument with your mother."

"Don't start with me, Wilson."

"I'm not. I just don't understand why you're acting this way."

Wilson saw the anger flash in Thurlow's eyes. "I don't remember asking you for your opinion."

"Hey, I'm not trying to . . ." But Wilson didn't know what to say, so he finally shut up.

Thurlow looked out at the field. He let it go, too. Thurlow's mom was standing in the first base coach's box. She was clapping and yelling to Jeremy Lim as he came up to bat.

Jeremy jumped on the first pitch and hit a little blooper between first and second. The right fielder came up fast but then fumbled the ball long enough to let Tracy race all the way around to third. Gloria, at the opposite end of the dugout, stood up and shouted, "Way to go, Trace! Nice baserunning!"

Wilson was thinking the Scrappers might make something out of this inning after all.

And then he noticed that Adam was still in the on-deck circle, swinging at phantom pitches, not even aware of what was happening on the field. Wilson couldn't help but laugh. Adam was a good guy, but he *was* strange.

Finally, the umpire called, "Come on, batter, let's go." Adam looked a little startled, but then he hurried over to the plate.

"What an idiot," Thurlow said. He leaned forward and spit in the dirt.

"That's just the way he is, Thurlow. But the guy can throw the ball."

"Sometimes."

Adam worked the count to 2 and 2, and then he lifted a fly to shallow left field. The left fielder jogged under it for the easy grab. At least that was only the second out, and Tracy was still on. . . .

And then Tracy took off for the plate.

The left fielder was caught off guard for a moment, but he recovered and made the easy throw home. With Tracy's good speed, she actually made the play close. She had the guts, too, to slam hard into the catcher. But the catcher hung on to the ball, and Tracy was out.

"This is nuts," Thurlow said. "No one knows what they're doing out there."

That seemed a little too close to the truth. Wilson let his breath out. He had already put his shin guards on. Now he grabbed his chest protector. He didn't like what he was hearing. Everyone was mumbling about Tracy. There was too much of that on this team: everyone on one another's back all the time.

But the loudest criticism came from Tracy's best friend, Gloria, who met her on the way back to the dugout. "What was that all about? Who gave you a signal to tag up?"

Tracy didn't look up as she stepped into the dugout and grabbed her glove.

Gloria followed her. "Aren't you going to answer?"

Tracy finally turned around and looked Gloria in the eye. "I thought I could make it. Okay?"

"I guess that's the problem. You *thought,* and you're not good at that."

Tracy stepped close, right into Gloria's face. "The next time I want your opinion will be the first time. Okay?"

Coach Carlton had walked over from the coach's box. "Hey, come on," he said. "Let's not start that, Gloria. Do you hear me?"

"Yeah," she grumbled, and she walked away.

"All right. Let's just get out there and play some defense," the coach yelled, and he clapped his hands.

Wilson was about to head for the plate when he heard Thurlow say, "Hey, Wilson, what about Gloria? Are you going to tell me that *she's* not a loser?"

Wilson came close to telling Thurlow who the biggest loser was, but he held back. He wondered how much longer he could do that. Thurlow's attitude was getting hard to take.

CHAPTER TWO

Wilson soon found that he had other worries besides Thurlow. Adam threw his first couple of pitches into the dirt and then sailed one way high. Wilson yelled, "Take it easy, Adam. Just chuck it in here." Adam nodded, looking confident, but threw another one in the dirt—and walked the batter.

Wilson could already hear the grumbling in the infield—most of it coming from Gloria. "Come on, Adam. Throw strikes," she moaned.

Wilson called a time-out and jogged out to the pitcher's mound. Adam looked puzzled. "I don't know what's happening. The ball feels heavy. Do you think there's something wrong with it?"

Wilson handed the ball to Adam. "It's the same ball," he said. "Maybe your arm is getting tired. Do you think you can keep going?"

Adam nodded. "Yeah. I'm okay. It's just that something weird is going on with the ball. You know what I mean?" He had that spacey look in his eyes—maybe a little more than usual.

"Look, Adam," Wilson said, "don't worry about working the corners. Just throw the ball over the plate and let the defense back you up." Wilson patted Adam on the shoulder and then ran back to the plate.

Robbie, from third base, shouted, "You're all right, Adam. Fire away."

Ollie Allman, the first baseman—and backup pitcher—yelled, "Get these guys out, Adam. I don't want to pitch." And the problem was, he really meant it.

Adam's first pitch to the next batter came in a little high, but the ump called it strike one. The next one was higher. Ball one. And the two after that were even higher than the ones before. Wilson had to jump to get the last one.

Wilson wasn't just worried about Adam. This was the point where the whole team could blow up. Gloria wasn't saying much, but a couple of times he had heard her mumble, "Oh, man," way too loud. Adam had to have heard her, and Coach Carlton, too.

The Coach had made it very clear that he wouldn't let Gloria work her teammates over—the way she sometimes had in the past. Wilson hoped Gloria wouldn't go too far and get herself booted out of the game.

The next pitch was probably low, but the batter chased it and missed, and the count was full. Tracy shouted from second base, "All right, Adam. Show this guy your heat!"

But the next pitch seemed to float to the plate. The batter got around on it, and he smacked a grounder to the left side of the in-field.

The ball skipped toward Gloria, and it looked like a routine out—maybe a double play. Gloria charged the ball as Tracy moved to cover second. But seeing the chance for a double play, Gloria tried to scoop the ball up on the run. The ball slipped under her glove and into the outfield.

Trent Lubak sprinted in from left field, grabbed the ball, and held the batter to a single. The runner on first had moved all the way around to third.

The Hot Rods' dugout was going crazy. Some of the players were really giving Gloria a hard time. "Hey, Gloria, use your mouth next time. It's bigger than your glove."

Wilson thought she almost deserved what she got. If she had taken her time, she could have made the easy force at second. At least maybe she would keep her mouth shut about Adam now.

Adam's next pitch hit the ground two feet in front of the plate. Wilson tried to knock it down, but it bounced over his shoulder and crashed against the backstop. He ripped off his mask, chased after it, turned and threw to Adam, who had charged from the mound to cover the plate.

Adam made the catch, but the runner dived headfirst ahead of the tag.

Safe!

By then the runner at first had jogged over to second. And still, the Hot Rods had no outs.

Wilson put his hands on his hips and dropped his head. He should have been able to block the ball. That was his job.

Adam was really rattled now, too. He finally walked the batter, and that brought Coach

Carlton to the mound. He called Ollie over to pitch and had Thurlow take over at first base.

Adam said, "Sorry, Coach, but I think you need to check the ball. It soaked up some water or something." He wandered off to the bench and sat down.

Thurlow, meanwhile, walked to first base. He stood near the bag with his arms folded over his chest. He hardly watched what was going on.

Ollie gave up a hit to the first batter he faced, and another run scored. But then he settled down. He got a strikeout and a force-out at second. And then the Hot Rods' tough little second baseman, a boy named Richie Thatcher, slapped a hard shot to Robbie, at third.

Robbie made a good stop and came up firing, but he threw the ball low. It was a tough catch, but Thurlow made it look easy. He scooped the ball up on the short hop—no problem. And the Scrappers were off the field.

Thurlow walked all the way back to the dugout, never even breaking into a trot. When the other players told him what a good stop he had made, he acted as though he hadn't heard them.

The Scrappers' offense was pathetic for the next couple of innings, and their defense wasn't much better. Wilson struck out twice. Luckily, the Hot Rods were just as bad, and going into the bottom of the seventh inning, the Scrappers were still only behind 4 to 2.

Chad Corrigan, now in the lineup for Martin, was up to bat first. That meant Wilson would be up fifth, but he didn't hold out much hope of the inning lasting that long.

As Chad walked to the plate, the sun was disappearing behind Mount Timpanogos in Utah's Wasatch Range. The heat had let up a little. Wilson thought maybe the shadows in the outfield would make it hard for the outfielders to see the ball. But someone had to knock it out there first, and he didn't think Chad had the swing to do it.

It appeared that Chad agreed, because he let the first two pitches go by. Luckily, he got ahead in the count, 2 to 0.

But the next two pitches were fat and down the middle, and still Chad didn't swing. With the count at 2 and 2, Oates took off his hat and wiped the sweat from his forehead.

Tracy cupped her hands around her mouth

and hollered, "What are you sweating for, Jake? Scared?"

Wilson was grateful that Tracy was at least aiming her attitude at the other team. But the coach didn't like taunting either.

The next pitch was high and inside. Chad ducked his head and turned, but the ball thudded hard against his shoulder. He grabbed the shoulder and bent over, obviously in pain.

Coach Carlton ran toward the plate. A few seconds went by, and all the Scrappers stood and waited. But then Chad waved the coach off, swung his arm around a couple of times, and trotted to first base. The Scrappers all cheered.

When Chad reached the base, he turned around and grinned. Then he pointed to his head.

Robbie was standing next to Wilson. "Did you see that?" he asked.

"He did it on purpose," Gloria said. "Now, that's cool."

The whole team reacted. Wilson felt a sudden surge of excitement, and he knew everyone else felt it, too. They were making more noise than they had in several innings.

"Come on, Jer. Get on base!" Trent was screaming. "We can still win this game."

Jeremy turned and called back, "I think I'll use my bat—if you don't mind."

It wasn't really that funny, but everyone in the dugout laughed. Jeremy was always so quiet. He had never said anything like that before.

Wanda whomped a couple of kids on the back. "*Crunch* that ball, Jeremy!" she was yelling.

Thurlow was the only one who wasn't getting involved in all this. He was in the on-deck circle, down on one knee. He didn't laugh; didn't say a word.

The enthusiasm fell off a little when Jeremy popped out on the first pitch, but Wilson shouted loud when Thurlow stepped into the box. That got everyone going again. Wilson just hoped Thurlow would concentrate and give it his best shot.

Thurlow stepped into the box, rested the bat on his shoulder, and just stood there—as though he were waiting for a bus, not a pitch.

Still, everyone knew what Thurlow could do. Oates looked nervous.

The first pitch was low, but Thurlow lashed at it anyway, and he made solid contact. Wilson's breath caught in his throat. The ball sailed high and long toward right field. It looked like it had a chance to get out of the park. But the ball was slicing to the right. It dropped over the fence and for a moment . . .

"Foul ball!" the ump called.

One of the Hot Rods yelled, "All right. That's just a big strike." But Oates had to know he had barely skinned by that time. Wilson could see that most of the confidence the Hot Rods had shown in the beginning of the game was now gone.

The next pitch was even lower, but again Thurlow took a long, powerful swing. And again the ball sailed foul. Chad, who had broken toward second, had to go back. Wilson could tell he wanted to run; he was expecting Thurlow to belt one.

Coach Carlton shouted out to Thurlow, "Don't make it easy for him, Thurlow. Make him throw strikes." Thurlow had stepped out of the box, and he actually seemed to pay attention. He might have even given a little nod.

Wanda shouted, "Thurlow, you wait for your pitch now. Quit swinging at those low ones!"

That was a mistake, and Wilson knew it immediately. Thurlow shot an angry look at his mother. Then he turned around, stepped into the box, and stood straight up again. The pitch came in at the knees, and Thurlow didn't even move his bat off his shoulder. The ump called strike three, and Thurlow glared at his mom all the way back to the dugout.

The Scrappers were completely silent when Thurlow walked into the dugout. Coach Carlton clapped him on the back, but he didn't say anything. Wanda looked mad enough to kill.

Wilson was glad to have an excuse to get out of the dugout. He grabbed a bat and walked to the on-deck circle. He was up after Robbie, but everything had changed now. Wilson expected Robbie to make the third out and end the game.

And the Hot Rods had come back to life. They were the ones talking it up now.

Robbie looked nervous. He eyed the first pitch, almost swung, and then held up. But the umpire called it a strike.

Wilson looked up in the bleachers. His parents hadn't made it to the game this time, but a lot of the Scrappers' families were there. They were still cheering, but not as loudly as they had been a few minutes before.

Wilson saw Robbie clench his jaw tight and step back into the box. He took a nice cut at the next pitch, but he hit the ball off the end of his bat. It dribbled down the first base line.

The first baseman and the pitcher both charged the ball. The pitcher got to it first, turned, and made a good throw. But the second baseman was a little late covering the bag. He stabbed at the ball, held it for an instant, and then dropped it.

Robbie shot by. Safe.

It took Wilson a moment to realize what had happened. The game wasn't over. He was up in the bottom of the seventh, with two outs, the team down by two runs, and with two men on base. He would either be a hero or a goat in the next few seconds.

He felt the pressure, and he didn't like it. Sure, he'd hit a home run, but he'd struck out every other time. As he walked to the plate, he could only think about how terrible he'd feel if he struck out again.

He was hardly concentrating and didn't react when the first pitch buzzed by him.

"Strike one!"

The shouts from the Hot Rods' infield brought him back to focus. "You've got him frozen now, Jake!" Thatcher yelled.

Wilson stepped out of the box and took a deep breath. Then he stepped back in and stared down the pitcher. He was going to have a good at bat, win or lose.

The next pitch was a ball, inside, and Wilson let it go. But although the pitch after that *seemed* outside, the ump called it a strike.

Wilson told himself he had to keep his head in, not chase any bad pitches. But he couldn't let anything close go by either.

Oates reared back and threw a thunderbolt, but it was outside this time. Wilson started to swing but held up. The count was even, 2 and 2, and Wilson had yet to swing.

Oates seemed frustrated. Wilson knew he wanted to get this game over with. *Maybe he'll serve this one up*, he thought.

When the ball left Oates's hand, Wilson saw it all the way, a little off-speed and straight as an arrow. He picked up his front foot, stepped forward, and swung as hard as he could. He felt awkward—all wrong—but he had hit the ball hard.

As he took off for first, he watched the left fielder running back—all the way to the fence.

Wilson slowed to a stop. This was going to be all or nothing. He followed the arc as the ball dropped toward the fence. The left fielder jumped, and for a moment Wilson wasn't sure what had happened.

Then he heard the scream, and he heard the umpire shout, "Home run!"

It took Wilson a second to realize he had to start running again. He had just won the game!

CHAPTER THREE

As Wilson pedaled his bike down the street, he soaked up the morning sun. He was still feeling the glory of the big win the night before. It was a pleasure to go to baseball practice today.

After the game the players had all been talking up the team, saying how good the Scrappers could be. Robbie and Trent even said they thought the team had a chance to win the league championship.

And everyone said it was Wilson who was leading the way. He was their long-ball hitter. The RBI man.

Wilson wanted to believe all of that stuff about the team, but he had his doubts. Pitching was a problem. Neither Adam nor Ollie could get the ball over the plate consistently. Against the better teams, those guys would have a hard time.

Also, it seemed like the Scrappers couldn't get through an inning without making an error. Even Gloria fouled up plays sometimes, and she was probably their best infielder.

The team wasn't scoring many runs either. If it hadn't been for Wilson's two homers, the Scrappers wouldn't have had any runs at all against the Hot Rods.

What Wilson did hope was that the win might bring the players a little closer together. At the end of the game they had actually acted like a team. But that wasn't usually the case. Thurlow was part of the problem, and Gloria's mouth didn't help. How could they be real teammates if they didn't even like one another?

At least Wilson felt pretty good about himself. He didn't have much experience at catching, but he got the job done most of the time. He'd only messed up once the night before. And even though he struck out more than he wanted to, he figured he was like most sluggers. They struck out because they swung hard—but they drove in runs when they connected.

Wilson bumped his bike over the curb and pumped across the grass into the park. He was at least ten minutes early for practice, but he could see Robbie, Ollie, and Trent over by the backstop. They were tossing a ball around, but they stopped when they saw Wilson ride up.

"Hey, here comes our superstar!" Robbie said. "The Hank Aaron of the Wasatch City League."

"How does it feel to be a hero?" Trent asked.

Wilson knew they were ribbing him, but it still felt good. After all, he couldn't deny it: he had been the hero. From now on, he could go to bat with more confidence.

"Somebody had to bail you guys out," Wilson joked. He dumped his bike by the fence and pulled his catcher's mitt from the handlebars.

"We'll get on base," Trent said. "You just keep bringing us home. We're going to show some teams what we can do."

Robbie gave Wilson a little slug in the shoulder. "Hey, can you believe what's happening? When we rounded all these kids up, we didn't know we were putting a good team together."

"All we cared about was having a chance to play," Wilson said.

"If Thurlow would get serious, this team

could be like the '61 Yankees. You two are our Mantle and Maris."

But as Trent tossed the ball to Wilson, he said, "We've got to cut down on the errors. But I'm serious; I think we can be good."

Maybe that was true. If everyone was willing to work hard, maybe the Scrappers could solve their problems. It was hard for Wilson not to get excited when the guys were talking this way.

The other players started arriving soon after that. Before long, Wilson saw Coach Carlton get out of his old pickup. By the time he walked across the park to the baseball diamond, the whole team was there—except Thurlow, of course, who was late again.

Everyone was in a great mood this morning. When the coach started the players out with some infield work, they played better than usual. The coach was upbeat, too. He didn't give any pep talks, but he was constantly teaching, reminding the players of fundamentals. "That's right," he would say when someone made a good pickup. "But set your feet before you throw. Try it again."

Wilson thought everyone was listening, too.

He saw them trying hard to do what the coach said.

When infield practice ended, the coach had the players run a lap around the park. While they were running, Wilson saw Wanda park her old Toyota next to the coach's truck. When she and Thurlow got out of the car, they both looked upset, like they had been doing battle that morning.

Coach Carlton started batting practice and had Wilson get behind the plate to work on his catching. Wilson watched as Thurlow walked to right field, not bothering to apologize or explain to Coach Carlton why he was late.

It was Wanda who walked over and said, "I'm sorry we're late. It was all I could do to get that boy out of bed this morning."

Wilson was close enough to hear the coach say, "Wanda, is there anything I can do to help?"

"I don't know," she answered. "I hope you can be patient with him. If he ever makes up his mind to play, you'll see things you can't believe from a boy his age."

"That might be so," the coach said. "But I can't baby him along forever."

"What he wants is for you to kick him off the team," Wanda said. "But I wouldn't let him off the hook that way. I just wish you could find a way to challenge him—so he'd want to show you what he can do."

The coach nodded. Then he glanced over and saw that Wilson was close enough to hear. He turned and shouted, "All right, let's have a batter. Jeremy, why don't you go first?"

Jeremy hustled in and grabbed a bat. As he took his strokes, the coach talked to him about holding his bat still, keeping his shoulders level.

The coach also advised Wilson on his catching. "Wilson, you're back on your heels too much. Stay up on the balls of your feet."

Wilson tried to follow Coach Carlton's instructions, but he had a hard time keeping his balance when he crouched that way. On the other hand, he knew that when he settled back on his heels, he had to bend too far forward—and he couldn't react to wild pitches as quickly. But knowing was one thing and doing was another.

Coach Carlton threw a couple of really low balls, probably on purpose. Wilson stopped one of them, but the other one skipped under his glove and rolled all the way to the backstop.

"Turn your mitt over, Wilson. When the ball comes in that low, turn it heel up, and put the tip right on the ground so nothing can get under it."

Coach Carlton threw a few more low ones, and Wilson did as he was told. The ball didn't get past him, but a couple of times it rolled up his glove onto his chest, and he had to hustle to control it. "That's okay," Coach Carlton reassured him. "At least you're keeping the ball in front of you. You'll get so you can catch that way." Wilson was glad that the coach thought he was improving.

Tracy hit next, and the coach gave her some good advice about striding toward the mound—and not "stepping in the bucket," as he called it. She started meeting the ball better after that.

Coach Carlton had all the kids bat, and then he finally waved to Thurlow. "Come on in, Thurlow. Let's see you take a few cuts."

Thurlow strolled in from the outfield, taking his time. He crossed the infield, tossed his glove on the ground, and picked up the nearest bat.

"Well, Thurlow, you look psyched to be here," Wilson said sarcastically.

"Yeah. Who would want to sleep in when a guy can be out here with all his best friends?"

His tone wasn't friendly, but at least he had spoken.

Coach Carlton tossed a few pitches, and Thurlow knocked most of them deep into the outfield—or over the fence. But the coach started increasing his speed and moving the pitches around. Thurlow had some problems handling the coach's better stuff. He foul tipped some and whiffed completely a few times.

Wilson watched Thurlow change his stance. He took the bat off his shoulder, opened his stance a little wider, got himself ready. He started to stroke the ball better—even when the coach was humming the ball pretty hard.

But Wilson was still having his troubles. He wasn't used to catching a pitcher with that much speed. He dropped a lot of balls and let a couple of pitches skip past him.

Coach Carlton kept offering advice to Wilson, but he didn't say a word to Thurlow. Wilson tried to do what the coach told him. He spread his feet a little farther apart, and that did seem to help with his balance. But then the coach threw some pitches outside, and those got by him.

"You can't just reach backhanded," the coach yelled to Wilson. "You have to move your whole body and get in front of the ball. You'll at least knock it down that way."

Wilson felt like those Russian dancers he had seen on TV—bouncing around in a crouch position. It just wasn't that easy.

He was also beginning to feel like he wasn't such a star at this game after all. He still had plenty to learn and to master.

But then the coach said something really surprising. "Okay, Thurlow, three more pitches. Let's see if I can strike you out."

Thurlow laughed. He glanced back at Wilson and said, "This poor guy doesn't know how old he is."

This time, when Thurlow took his stance, he looked like a ballplayer. He set his feet, held his bat back and ready, and he focused his eyes right on the coach.

The first pitch didn't seem to have much on it. Wilson thought Thurlow would kill it. But the ball broke as it reached the plate. Thurlow took a hard swing—and missed.

But he seemed to like that. He laughed, and then he said, "Try that again. I didn't expect a curveball."

But the coach called back, "I'm not going to tell you what pitch I'm throwing. How dumb do you think I am?"

"Dumb enough," Thurlow whispered, but he got ready again.

This time the pitch had some mustard on it, and it was in on Thurlow's hands. He got around on the pitch pretty well, but he hit it off the handle and popped it foul.

"Strike two," the coach said.

"It takes three," Thurlow said, and he got set again.

This time the pitch was on the outside edge—and *hard*. Thurlow stepped into it and hammered it, deep to right field. It sailed way over the fence.

The coach nodded. "Not bad," he said. And then he smiled. "I guess I don't have the speed I used to have."

"Hey, you still got some," Thurlow said. Wilson actually heard some respect in his voice.

"Thurlow, why don't you get behind the

plate?" the coach said. "Let's let Wilson take some swings."

Surprisingly, Thurlow tossed his bat aside and started putting on the catcher's gear as Wilson removed it.

"That was a real *shot* you just hit," Wilson offered as he unstrapped his shin guards.

"Hey, who couldn't hit that old guy?"

"You missed a couple."

"I just wasn't taking him seriously at first."

Wilson thought about a few things he could have said to that, but he kept his mouth shut again.

CHAPTER FOUR

Wilson took a few practice swings and then stepped into the box. Robbie turned from third base and yelled to the outfielders, "Hey, move back. The big stick is up!"

Wilson laughed, but he felt some pressure. He had to hit a few long ones, especially following Thurlow's performance.

The coach tossed a nice pitch down the middle. Wilson stepped into it and took a big swing. *Crack!* The ball took off like a rocket, and Wilson couldn't keep a huge grin from spreading across his face.

Before he could even enjoy the satisfaction of seeing the ball land deep in center field, Coach Carlton said, "Nice hit, Wilson. But the same thing that gets you those long hits also causes a lot of strikeouts."

"I guess I swing too hard, don't I?" Wilson said.

"Well, yes. But there's more to it than that. You hold your bat high at first, but then, when the pitch is on the way, you drop it way down. That pulls your right shoulder down, too, and you swing up on the ball."

"Is that bad?"

"Sure. If your swing isn't timed perfectly, you miss, or you pop the ball up. If you can swing on the same plane as the ball, you're going to get a lot more hits. That means you have to keep those shoulders level."

Wilson was a little surprised. He thought he had taken a good cut. It had been over the center fielder's head, after all. And a few strikeouts and pop-ups were the price you paid to be a slugger.

The next pitch was right at Wilson's belt, and he launched it again. But this time he hit it higher in the air. Jeremy faded back and caught it.

"See what I mean?" the coach said. "That's just a long out. You got under the ball and hit it too high. You dropped your bat way down again."

Wilson thought maybe the coach had a point. He concentrated on his bat and his shoulders on the next pitch. But he swung and missed.

"That's better, Wilson!"

What? It hadn't felt better. It felt awkward, and he had missed the ball.

Thurlow muttered from behind, "Oh, yeah, great coaching."

Wilson kept trying to do what Coach Carlton told him, and he kept missing. "That's okay," the coach said. "I know it feels funny, but you've got to retrain your muscles. You're swinging under the ball because you're used to that upward slant in your swinging plane."

Wilson wasn't sure he understood that. He was getting frustrated. And Thurlow never stopped talking. "Yeah, Wilson, you've got to retrain your muscles so it'll feel natural when you miss."

Wilson wanted him to shut up, but he was starting to think Thurlow was right. Why didn't the coach just leave his swing alone? It had worked okay before, hadn't it?

Finally, after a lot of pitches, Wilson connected on some line drives, but the swing still felt awkward.

Coach Carlton said, "Once you get used to this, you won't strike out so much, Wilson. You've got some bad habits, so you might as well break them now, before you get older."

Wilson hoped that was true. But as he pedaled home after practice, he was still wondering. He had been a whole lot happier when he thought he was a hero.

Wilson spent the afternoon inside, reading. At first he kept thinking about batting practice and what Thurlow had said, but he finally got lost in his book, and the time slipped by. When he heard a knock on the door, he looked up to see his dad. "Mom's just starting dinner," Mr. Love said. "Do you want to play some catch?"

"Sure," Wilson said. He rolled off the bed. His father was funny about wanting to play catch. He really wasn't much of an athlete, but Wilson understood. This was his way of being close to his son. It was sort of funny—but Wilson didn't mind.

When they got outside, his dad took off his sport coat and folded it over a lawn chair. Then Wilson tossed the baseball to him. They threw the ball back and forth a few times before his dad asked, "How was practice today?"

Wilson shrugged. After zinging the ball back, he answered, "The coach worked with me on my hitting."

"That's one thing you don't have to worry about."

The ball sailed high, and Wilson had to jump to catch it. "Actually, I do. The coach thinks I strike out too much. He tried to change my swing. But now I feel all messed up. I think I might stick with what I was doing."

His dad nodded, but Wilson could tell he was thinking.

"Don't you think I should do that? I mean, I've been hitting a lot of homers."

His father seemed to give the idea some thought, and then he finally tossed the ball back. "When I was in my first year of graduate school, I took a class on *Beowulf*."

It was all Wilson could do not to roll his eyes. His dad was always talking about old books. He was a literature professor.

"I thought I knew *Beowulf* backward and forward—until I got my first paper back with a big red C on it. At first I was mad. Then I went and talked to my professor about it, and I raised a few questions. Before I got out of that office, I realized he knew more about Old English poetry than I *ever* would. He turned out to be my favorite professor, too—had a big influence on me."

Wilson threw the ball back and said, "Oh."

"What I'm saying, Wilson, is that you've got quite an opportunity. From everything I've heard, Coach Carlton really knows his baseball."

Wilson caught the ball and turned it in his glove a couple of times before throwing it back. "I know."

Mr. Love walked over to Wilson. "Son, everything I've accomplished in my life is due to taking advantage of opportunities that come along. I think you should take advantage of the one you've got right now."

Wilson nodded. He took the ball from his dad, and they walked into the house.

When the Scrappers took the field against the Pit Bulls on Friday night, the sun was already going down. That was fine with Wilson. Playing earlier in the evening was just too hot.

But Wilson was feeling more than one kind

of heat. Everyone on the team kept calling him their slugger—even though he'd been struggling at the plate all week in practice. Wilson was losing confidence, and it only added pressure to know that his teammates were counting on him so much.

The Pit Bulls were up first, and Wilson could soon see that he had more to worry about than just his hitting. Ollie was the starting pitcher, but his pitches were flying all over the place. Before the Scrappers got an out, Ollie had walked three batters and given up a two-run single.

The next batter came to the plate with runners on first and third. He was a guy Wilson had played flag football with. Wilson had never known his first name. Kids just called him "Boone." And that was the name printed in yellow letters on his dark blue jersey: BOONE'S PEST CONTROL. All the players on the team looked like Boone, too: strong, tough, and serious.

Ollie's first pitch was over the plate. Boone let it go—probably surprised Ollie could throw a strike. Wilson lobbed the ball back and yelled, "Nice pitch, Ollie. Keep it up."

Gloria was yelling, too. Wilson knew how frustrated she had to be, the way the game had started. But she wasn't cussing Ollie out—not yet, at least.

Ollie still looked nervous. His next two pitches took off on him, way high. Wilson felt lucky to jump up and catch both of them.

Ollie paced the mound and talked to himself. Wilson was sure that he was telling himself to bring the ball down. So as Ollie started his windup, Wilson squatted low. He half expected a pitch in the dirt.

It was a good guess: the ball angled down toward the ground, and Wilson flipped his glove heel up, the way Coach Carlton had taught him. But the ball ricocheted off home plate, skipped off his glove, and flew straight behind him. Wilson spun around and chased after it.

As he grabbed the ball, he heard Gloria shout, "Second base." Wilson twisted and fired the ball toward second, but he put way too much on it, and the ball sailed over Tracy's head into center field.

Jeremy charged in, fielded the ball, and threw home, but it was too late. The runner from third scored, and the runner from first kept going all the way to third.

Three runs in and there were still no outs.

Wilson smacked his thigh with his glove and kicked at the dirt. He wanted to crawl inside his catcher's mask and hide. It was bad enough not to make the stop on the ball, but he knew he had panicked after that. He had probably had no chance at second. Why had he listened to Gloria? He should have just held on to the ball.

Wilson could hear his mom and dad yelling from the bleachers. "That's all right, Wilson. You're doing fine." But that only made him feel worse.

Coach Carlton walked halfway to the plate and said, "Wilson, we're all right. It's still early." And Wilson tried to tell himself the coach was right. But he couldn't seem to calm down. He wasn't thinking clearly about his signals, and he dropped a couple of balls that hit him right in the glove.

At least Ollie was starting to find the plate. He got a pop-up for an out and then gave up a couple of hits. Two more runs scored, but at least he wasn't walking everybody.

Just when it seemed the Scrappers were going to be out of this game before it started, the Pit Bulls' right fielder hit a sharp grounder to Tracy. Tracy made the stop and fired to Gloria, who was charging to the bag. She dragged her foot over the bag for the out, then threw a bullet to first. Double play!

The Scrappers were finally out of the inning. They were down 5 to 0, but they all knew it could have been worse. They could score some runs now and get back in the game.

Wilson took off his catcher's gear. He wanted to get up to bat and make up for his mistake. But the Scrappers went down, one-two-three, and Wilson, who was fourth in the lineup tonight, had to get his equipment back on.

Ollie must have had a good talk with himself between innings—or maybe the coach gave him a tip. All Wilson knew was that Ollie's fastball was starting to pop. The first two Pit Bull batters made contact, but they hit looping fly balls for easy outs. The next batter fouled off a couple of pitches and then got caught looking when Ollie threw a heater right down the tube.

The Scrappers were talking it up this time when they ran back to the dugout. They all slapped Ollie on the back. And he was mumbling, probably congratulating himself.

CHAPTER FIVE

Wilson started peeling off his gear. He was feeling excited until Robbie said, "All right! Wilson's going to get one of those runs back right now. Just one swing of the bat."

Wilson didn't want that. He grabbed a bat and headed for home plate. He was trying to think what to do: try it the coach's way or his own.

He watched the first two pitches, both balls, and started to hope he could get on base without swinging. But he held his bat lower than he always had before, and he tried not to bend at the waist so much. He also thought about keeping his shoulders level, the way the coach had told him.

The next pitch was perfect, and Wilson triggered. He lashed hard at the ball and missed. Strike one.

"Come on, Wilson," the coach shouted. "Just meet the ball. Swing level."

Wilson knew he had reverted to his old habits. He also knew that he didn't want to strike out. This time he needed to remember what the coach had taught him.

The next pitch was just above his knees. He tried to take a smooth, level swing. But he swung under the ball.

Strike two.

And then he heard something he didn't expect. Thurlow yelled, "Just swing away, Wilson. Smack one." He didn't say, "Forget what the coach has been telling you," but Wilson knew that's what he meant.

As Wilson set up for the next pitch, he had no idea what he was going to do. The pitch was over the plate—the kind he had been able to smack a mile with his old swing.

He started to lash at the ball again, but he let off and stabbed, weakly.

Strike three.

Wilson wanted to slam the bat into the ground or chuck it into the backstop. He fumed all the way back to the dugout. But Coach Carlton patted him on the shoulder. "Your second swing was just right. Remember what you did."

Wilson could hardly believe what he was hearing.

Coach Carlton seemed to sense his frustration. "Don't worry. If you keep swinging that way, you'll get your hits. I promise."

Wilson didn't say a word. But he had to wonder. Maybe the coach was so old that he had a bunch of tired theories in his head. Maybe he was going to leave Wilson permanently messed up. But Wilson didn't want to think that. He purposefully sat down as far away from Thurlow as he could. He didn't want to talk to the guy.

The next few innings went the same way: the Scrappers struggled on defense but only gave up a couple more runs, and they struggled even more on offense. At least the Pit Bulls made a couple of errors in the fifth inning, and Gloria slammed a long double, up against the fence. Two runs scored, but then Trent struck out, and that was the end of the rally.

Wilson got up to bat twice more, and he concentrated on what the coach had taught him. But his timing was all off. He tried to swing easier, but mostly he just swung late. He struck out both times. The coach told him, "You're looking better all the time, Wilson."

Wilson was sorry, but that sounded like the stupidest thing he had ever heard.

The game went to the bottom of the seventh inning with the Scrappers down 7 to 2.

The good news was, the Pit Bulls' coach lifted his pitcher and put in a kid who didn't look nearly so tough. As the guy warmed up, he looked like he could throw strikes, but he was small and didn't have a lot of power. In the dugout, everyone was saying, "Okay, this is our chance."

But it was a slim chance. The bottom of the lineup was coming to the plate.

Cindy Jones was now in the game for Tracy. She was no power hitter, but she could handle a bat. She dug in like she meant business and swung at the first pitch. She hit a little fly ball over the head of the third baseman for a single.

The Scrappers woke up in the dugout.

Ollie came up next, and Adam shouted after him, "Come on, Ollie, keep it going!"

Wilson wanted to cheer for him, but he had a hard time getting excited. He still felt too rotten about the way his day had gone.

Ollie stepped in and took his strange stance. He held the bat very low, and he stood very straight. Wilson wondered why the coach didn't have something to say about that. But after taking a strike and a ball, Ollie knocked a hard grounder to the right side.

Cindy had to skip over the ball as she ran toward second. The ball shot past the first baseman and into right field.

Now the bench really started to talk it up. Two runners on, no outs, and Thurlow coming up to bat. Wilson finally found his voice. "Do it, Thurlow! Park one. We're still in this game."

Thurlow sauntered up to the plate, looking like he didn't know the score. He had been playing right field for two innings, but this was his first time at bat. Wilson could see that the pitcher was starting to fidget around, and the Pit Bulls' bench was pleading with him to throw some heat at Thurlow.

Wilson noticed that they knew Thurlow's name. They probably also knew what their pitcher was up against.

The Pit Bulls' coach came out of the dugout

and met the catcher and the pitcher at the mound. They didn't talk for long, and it was soon obvious that the pitcher had been told not to give Thurlow anything good to hit.

The first two pitches were outside. Wilson saw the strategy: try to get Thurlow to chase one. If he wouldn't do it, let him walk, but at all cost, avoid the long ball.

But Wilson saw something else, too. Thurlow wasn't just standing there. He had taken his good stance, and he was watching the pitcher carefully.

The entire Scrappers' team was standing up, yelling. The crowd in the bleachers was roaring, too, the parents all cheering for their kids.

The next pitch was still outside, but the umpire called it a strike. Thurlow gave him a dirty look, and then he dug in again. He had never looked so determined.

The next pitch was low and outside, but close again, and Thurlow took a big cut. And missed.

Coach Carlton clapped his hands. "Don't make it easy on him, Thurlow," he yelled. "Make him throw strikes."

The pitcher took a long time between pitches. The ballpark was breathlessly quiet by the time he went into his windup.

From where Wilson was standing, it seemed as though the pitcher had decided to bust Thurlow inside. He saw Thurlow start to bail out. But the ball must have broken over the plate—a curveball.

Thurlow looked stunned. "That ball was inside," he barked at the umpire. But he didn't argue long, and as he walked back to the dugout, he tossed the bat away, almost casually. Wilson knew he didn't want anyone to think he cared.

A switch seemed to turn off in the Scrappers' dugout. They all sat down and quietly watched Jeremy ground out to the second baseman. And they weren't cheering at all by the time Trent hit a solid shot to left—right at the left fielder.

The game was suddenly over, and the Scrappers had lost.

The players lined up and shook hands with the Pit Bulls. "Good game," Wilson told them, and he meant it. At least they weren't a bunch of loudmouths.

Coach Carlton told the kids he was proud of their effort. "You got off to a bad start in the first inning, but after that you played them tough."

That was true, but they had still lost by five runs. The Scrappers broke up and headed home. They didn't seem to have much to say to one another.

Wilson walked alone toward his bike. His parents had driven to the game and would be waiting at home. When he heard someone jogging up behind him, he looked around and saw Gloria.

"Hey, Wilson, tough night, huh?"

She fell into stride with him. "Yeah," he said. But he didn't really feel like talking.

"Don't worry about it, Wilson. I know what you're doing wrong." Wilson got to his bike and started working on his combination lock. He was hardly paying attention when Gloria said, "See, you're slowing down your swing, but you're still waiting as long as you used to. That's throwing your timing off."

"Maybe so," Wilson said. He pulled his bike from the rack and got ready to go.

But Gloria stayed after him. "The coach is

right about taking a smooth stroke. But you have to get it started sooner."

Wilson threw his leg over his bike, and he finally looked at Gloria. "Okay. Thanks," he said.

And then he heard a voice behind him. "That's not the problem."

Gloria and Wilson both twisted around. It was Thurlow, standing a few feet away. "You don't know what you're talking about, Gloria, so why don't you just save it? What he needs to do is go back to his natural swing."

Gloria looked a little like a pit bull herself when she got mad. She stepped up to Thurlow, with her lips pulled back, her teeth bared. "Oh, all of a sudden you care about baseball? Is that what you're telling us? It's too bad you didn't care in the seventh inning! Nice strikeout."

Wilson glanced around to see that Robbie and Trent and Ollie were walking toward the bike rack. They stopped and listened. Farther away, Tracy and Cindy were watching.

This is the last thing this team needs, Wilson thought, but before he could say anything to settle the argument, the ballpark lights went out.

All of a sudden everything was very dark.

Wilson could see only outlines of Gloria and Thurlow, and he couldn't see the other players at all. And then he realized that Thurlow was walking off into the dark, not even bothering to argue with Gloria.

After a moment Gloria and the others did the same, and Wilson was left alone.

CHAPTER SIX

The mechanical arm released, catapulting the baseball toward Wilson. He took a huge, home run swing . . . and missed.

He had swung so hard he almost fell down. But that was only because he was sick of taking "smooth, level" swings and never getting solid wood on the ball.

The light on the machine went out, and Wilson, breathing hard and soaked in sweat, walked to the back of the cage. He took three quarters from the top of a stack and slid them into the slot.

He'd been at the batting cages all morning. It was a Saturday, and he didn't have practice, so he figured he'd do some work on his own. But the sun was getting hot now, and his swing was actually getting worse.

The pitching machine made a whirring sound as it started up again, and Wilson got into his crouch. He finally thought about what Gloria had told him. Maybe she was right.

He forced himself to swing sooner, but he got no look at the ball that way. It was like swinging in the dark. At least before, he had been popping the ball up sometimes, or fouling it off. Now, he was missing completely. After about the tenth try—and getting nothing but air—he spun away from the plate. He raised his bat and was about to smash it against the wire fence.

A voice cut him off. "Hey, go easy on the equipment." Wilson turned to see Thurlow leaning against the back of the cage, looking in.

"What are you doing here?" Wilson asked.

The pitching machine kept going, whacking baseballs into the plastic tarp at the back of the cage. They were hitting right next to Thurlow, but he didn't flinch. "I called your house. Your mom said you were over here."

"You want to hit some balls?"

"Naw."

This was strange. Wilson had no idea what

Thurlow was doing there. But he didn't ask. He got back in the batter's box, and he told himself to settle down, to go back to the level swing. He met a couple pretty well, but most of the time he was swinging under the ball, popping it up, or missing it.

Thurlow didn't make any comments about his hitting, but after a time he said, "Look who's coming. Just what I *didn't* want."

Wilson stepped out of the box. Robbie and Trent waved and then headed toward Wilson's cage.

"Hey, guys," Robbie said. "I guess you were thinking the same as us."

"How come you're not batting, Thurlow?" Trent asked.

Thurlow didn't look at Trent. "Why should I?" he asked, his voice sounding more bored than hostile.

Trent and Robbie obviously didn't know how to react. Neither said a word for a time, and then Robbie looked at Wilson. "Hey, you're wasting your quarters," he said. "You've still got some pitches left."

"That's all right," Wilson said. The last thing

he wanted to do was swing with all these guys watching him.

"I thought I saw what you were doing wrong last night," Robbie said. "You're trying to swing level, but you're still dropping your right shoulder. That makes you—"

"Lay off," Thurlow interrupted. "Everybody's telling Wilson what to do. He was doing fine before the coach started messing with his mind."

Robbie was obviously surprised by Thurlow's anger. "I was just trying to help."

"Wilson doesn't need your help." Thurlow turned to Wilson. "Just go back to what you were doing. Forget all this other stuff."

Wilson leaned the bat against the fence as the last pitch smacked the back of the cage. "I've tried going back to my old swing. It doesn't work. Everything I do feels wrong now."

Robbie shoved his hands in his pockets. "I don't know, Wilson," he said, "Maybe you should just—"

"Robbie, I told you to shut up," Thurlow said. "He doesn't need your *baseball card* coaching tips."

Robbie looked furious. "What I was going to say—before you cut me off—was that maybe Wilson should stop worrying so much. Just quit practicing and let his swing happen."

"When did you get so brilliant, Robbie? That's what I've been saying all along."

Robbie stepped toward Thurlow. "What do you mean, '*saying* all along'? You don't *say* anything. You just sit on the bench and watch."

Wilson didn't know what to do. He could see a fight coming, and that was the last thing he wanted. He stepped out of the cage and walked over to the guys, but he worried that if he stepped in to stop them, they'd think he was taking sides.

Thurlow leaned in close to Robbie. "Listen, *punk*, don't talk trash at me! You're the guy who let a *girl* beat you out for your position."

Robbie took a step back and shook his head. "You're such a waste, Thurlow."

"What?" Thurlow stepped up close again, bumping his chest into Robbie's chin.

"You're a *waste*," Robbie repeated, and he didn't give an inch. "You're the best athlete on our team, but you don't *try*. You could carry us on your backs if you wanted to, but you're playing some little kindergarten game with your mother."

Thurlow slammed both his hands into Robbie's chest and sent him stumbling backward.

Wilson had had enough. He stepped in between the two boys and yelled, "What's wrong with you two? You've got nothing to fight about!"

Wilson looked at Thurlow and then turned to look at Robbie. Both guys still looked angry. "Let's just lay off all this stuff," Wilson said.

Robbie shrugged. "That's fine with me. I don't want any trouble," he said.

But Thurlow's eyes lost none of their hardness. "See you around," he said, and he walked away.

"This is stupid," Wilson yelled after him. "Why can't we all just play some baseball together?"

Thurlow didn't answer, didn't even look back. Wilson still couldn't figure out why he had come over in the first place.

"What the heck is his problem?" Trent asked.

"Hey, he's a good guy," Wilson said. "He's just mad right now."

"He's *always* mad."

"No, he isn't. He never used to be like that. Everybody just needs to cut him a little slack."

"Oh, yeah. Right," Robbie said. "You get just as tired of his attitude as anyone."

Wilson didn't know what to say. That did sum things up pretty well. But it was frustrating. Every time things started to go a little better, something fouled it all up again.

Wilson walked his bike up the block toward his house. He had a bad headache. He was looking down as he walked and almost didn't see his mom's old station wagon backing out of the driveway. He had to make a quick stop. "Mom, watch where you're going! You almost killed me."

Mrs. Love rolled down the window. "I saw you, honey," she said. "You were the one with your chin on your chest, not looking. Batting practice didn't go so well, I take it."

Wilson shrugged. He didn't want to get into it.

"What are you doing now?"

"I don't know. Nothin'."

"Why don't you come grocery shopping with me?"

"I don't think so, Mom," Wilson said, but he didn't walk away.

"Oh, come on. No one is home. You don't want to sit here alone all afternoon. Come with me."

"Okay." He pushed his bike up the lawn and put it in the garage. Then he walked back to the car.

As his mother backed out, she started on a monologue about her flowers. Something about the heat burning them up. Wilson stared out the window, not really listening.

Suddenly, he realized his mother had said something to him. "What?" he asked.

"What's going on, Wil?"

Wilson hesitated. But he actually did want to talk to her. So he told his story quickly, leaving out most of the details. He couldn't hit anymore, and he didn't know why. Everybody had a different opinion about what was wrong. Thurlow was being a pain in the rear, but the team didn't have to be so down on him. And now, Robbie and Thurlow had almost gotten into a fight— which was stupid, since they were both good guys. "The dumb thing is," he said, as his mom was parking at Smith's Food King, "we've got a lot of good players. And Thurlow and Gloria and Robbie are probably the three best. But they're all mad at each other. No wonder we got beat last night."

"You're a good player, too, Wil. You won that one game almost by yourself."

"Yeah. Back when I could still hit." Wilson let out a deep sigh and leaned his head against the seat.

His mom smiled and patted him on the arm. "I'm so proud of you, Wilson Love," she said.

Wilson rolled his eyes. Parents were always proud of you when your life was falling apart. He suspected they taught that in parents' school: "When your kids are miserable, tell 'em you're proud of them. Works every time."

"I know how much you want to be a great baseball player, and I know how disappointed you are that you struck out every time last night."

What kind of pep talk is this? Wilson wondered.

"But here's what impresses me. You're more worried about the team than you are about your own batting problems."

Wilson could see where she was going now, but he wasn't sure she was right.

"That makes you a leader, Wilson. And that's why I'm proud of you."

A leader? Wilson wasn't so sure. He did want to settle the differences between Thurlow and the rest of the team, but so far, he hadn't accomplished a thing.

Wilson got out of the car and trailed his mother through the grocery store. And he thought about the things she had said. He doubted he was a leader. After all, people listened to leaders. But she was right about one thing: he was even more concerned about the trouble among his teammates than he was about his swing. And he was plenty worried about his swing.

Maybe that did mean something. At least he felt a *little* better. And his headache was gone.

CHAPTER SEVEN

Wilson sat down on the grass to stretch out his hamstrings. All the kids were showing up for Monday's practice, and one by one they started their own stretching exercises. That was something the coach had taught them all to do.

Robbie walked over and sat down next to Wilson. He folded his leg behind him in a hurdler's position, then leaned backward to stretch out his thighs. "Have you talked to Thurlow since Saturday?"

"No," Wilson said quickly. He didn't want Robbie to think that he was on Thurlow's side. But then, he didn't want Thurlow to think he was on Robbie's side either. "I'm sorry Thurlow was such a jerk, Robbie."

Robbie reached for his toes, grunted as he put a little pressure on his stretch, and then said,

"Don't worry about it. It's not your fault."

But Wilson *was* worried about it. To some degree, he felt responsible for Thurlow's actions. After all, Wilson was the one who had gotten Thurlow to sign up for summer baseball in the first place.

Wilson stood up and shook out his legs. Gloria was nearby, also stretching. She was talking to Tracy, but Tracy didn't seem to be paying much attention. Of course, Gloria talked so loud everyone could hear her. "The Stingrays aren't any good," she was saying. "We can beat those guys."

Trent wasn't much for stretching. He had done a few squats, and now he was waiting for Robbie and the other guys. He socked his fist into his glove and said, "I watched the Stingrays play. They've got *nothing*."

"We actually have some pretty fair players on this team," Gloria said. "Sometimes Ollie and Adam are halfway decent pitchers. I never thought that would happen. All the work Coach Carlton puts in with those guys is paying off."

Ollie and Adam weren't that far away, and Wilson knew they had heard Gloria. They glanced at each other and smiled. It was not exactly high praise, but from Gloria, it was more than they expected.

"And you know who's really gotten better?" Tracy didn't respond, so Gloria answered her own question. "Jeremy."

Tracy looked up. She nodded and glanced at Jeremy, who was still stretching out just a few feet away. He was pretending not to listen.

Gloria continued the scouting report. "He hasn't overrun a fly ball in a long time. Except for that one in the last game."

Wilson shook his head, but he smiled. Gloria did seem to mean well, even if her compliments sounded more like insults. At least she was trying to be positive, and Wilson had the feeling she was doing it on purpose. Maybe she had given some thought to the things the coach had told her.

"We have a lot of games left," Gloria said, and she stood up. She seemed to be speaking to everyone, and most of the players looked in her direction. "If we pull it together, we've still got a shot at winning the first-half championship. Maybe an outside shot, but you know . . . it could happen."

"That's right," Adam said. He was staring off at the clouds, as though he saw something out there that was quite fascinating. "Maybe we're not that great, but a lot of teams are just as bad as we are."

Some of the kids laughed. Adam had a strange way of saying things, but in his own way, he was showing some team spirit.

Robbie got up. "Adam's right!" he shouted. "There are a lot of teams that *stink* more than us!"

Everybody was laughing now, and Trent yelled, "Go, Scrappers!"

That started a chant. "Go, Scrappers. Go, Scrappers." Before long, every player was shouting. It was half in jest, but at least everyone was in on it, and all the bad feelings suddenly seemed to disappear. Wilson loved it.

About then Coach Carlton pulled up in his pickup. The players picked up the cheer even louder. When the coach got out of the truck, he grinned and waved his fist. "That's the spirit," he yelled to them.

It was a good moment.

The coach walked over and waited, and

gradually the kids quieted. When they did, he said, "Hey, that's exactly what we need on this team. Some enthusiasm." He hesitated for a moment, and then he added, "Let's work hard today. Take a lap, and then we'll do some infield practice first. We've got to cut down on all the errors we're making."

The players trotted off together, and someone picked up the cheer again. "Go, Scrappers!"

But Wilson had spotted something that made him stop yelling. Thurlow was standing in right field. For some reason, his mom wasn't there, and yet he had come on his own. That was a good sign. The only problem was, he must have seen—and heard—what was going on, and he hadn't bothered to walk over. Wilson had no idea what it was going to take to draw Thurlow into this team.

When the players completed their loop around the park, they sprinted the finish back to the pitcher's mound, where Coach Carlton was waiting. He sent the outfielders to center field, and he had Trent hit them some flies. Then he worked with the infield himself.

Practice went well. The coach kept drilling

the players on basic principles, and Wilson could see that, compared to the first practice, everyone was doing a lot better. His catching seemed a little better today, too. The coach had him work on making a quick move to the left or right on inside and outside pitches. Wilson did feel like he was getting the idea.

Batting was still a problem, though. He kept trying to do what Coach Carlton had told him to do, but the results weren't any better. He missed over and over again, and when he did make contact, he never seemed to drive the ball hard anymore. The coach kept saying, "That looks good, Wilson. Your swing is right. Now just watch the ball and meet it."

That actually happened a few times, but not enough to give Wilson much confidence.

No one was calling Wilson "slugger" anymore either. Wilson had worried about the pressure before. Now he knew that no one was expecting much out of him. That was even worse.

When Wilson finished at the plate, Coach Carlton called Thurlow in to take the last turn at bat. The whole team waited as Thurlow walked slowly in from the outfield. Wilson could feel that the resentment toward Thurlow was growing. He hated to see that happen, but he didn't know what he could do about it—unless Thurlow made some effort himself.

Coach Carlton served up a couple of fat pitches, which Thurlow drove hard. He wasn't messing around either. He was taking a good stance, looking alert. This little battle with the coach was the one thing that Thurlow seemed to find some interest in.

Coach Carlton gradually picked up the speed and movement of his pitches. Thurlow stayed with him, slamming lots of line drives, and even hitting a couple over the fence.

Eventually the coach came up with some hard pitches, even some curveballs, and Thurlow swung and missed a few times. When that happened, the coach would kid him. "I'm just an old man. I shouldn't ever be able to get one past you." Thurlow actually seemed to like that. He wouldn't say anything, but he would look intense and determined, and then go after the next pitch.

On the last pitch of practice, Thurlow hit a

bullet of a grounder toward Tracy. She took one step to her left, got down on the ball, and put her glove down. It looked like she was in perfect position, but the ball skipped out of her glove straight in the air. She was able to barehand it on one bounce, however, and get it to first quickly. In a game situation, she probably would have gotten the runner. It was not a bad play.

Coach Carlton told her, "Good job, Tracy. That was a hard shot, but you stayed with it." Then he sent the team on another jog around the park to finish out the practice. Gloria jogged up beside Tracy. "Hey, Trace, I saw what you did wrong on that last grounder."

Tracy gave Gloria a disgusted look, but Gloria had her head down and didn't notice. Wilson was jogging right behind them. He wanted to say, "Don't do this, Gloria. Don't mess up everything that's happened today." But he kept his mouth shut.

"You're getting down on the ball really well, but—"

Tracy suddenly picked up her pace, and Gloria had to hurry to catch up. "Hey, listen for a sec. I'm not putting you down. I just happened to see what you're doing wrong."

Tracy kept running.

"Trace, did you hear what I said? I just—"

Suddenly Tracy stopped. Wilson almost ran into her, and Gloria had to put on her brakes and then turn back around. By then Tracy was screaming, "Did I *hear* you? Are you kidding? Everybody can hear you!"

All the players broke off their run, and they all turned to see what was happening.

"I'm so sick of you telling me everything I do wrong," Tracy shouted.

Gloria looked shocked. She stood there, mouth slightly open, still breathing hard from the run.

"What makes you think *you* know everything?" Tracy yelled. "I've played this game as long as you have."

Gloria was still just staring at Tracy. She didn't say a word, and no one else did either. And then someone laughed.

Thurlow.

Gloria spun toward him, still with a confused look on her face.

Thurlow started to clap, slow and steady. "Tracy finally told you to shut up, Gloria. I've got to applaud that."

"I'll tell you who should shut up," Gloria screamed. "That's you!"

"Hey, I'm not the one with my mouth always flapping."

"That's right. You don't say *anything*. You're not part of our team. You're just a bench-warmer."

"I can outplay you any day of the week, and you know it."

"Oh, is that right? Then why don't you prove it? Right now, I don't even know why you bother showing up. No one would even notice if you just disappeared."

Thurlow took a step forward, and Wilson could see that he was raging. "We'd all notice if you didn't show up, Gloria. It'd be so nice and quiet."

Before either one could push this thing any further, Wilson jumped in. He pushed between the two, grabbed hold of Thurlow's shoulders, and said, "Come on, you two. Stop this."

Thurlow took a step back and pushed Wilson

away. "What's wrong with you, Wilson?" he said. "Stay out of this."

But the coach was on his way over. "Hey, what's going on?" he yelled. And then, as he came closer, "I can't believe this. Who started it?"

No one said a word.

"We just finished the best practice we've ever had. What's happening now?"

Wilson didn't know how to explain. No one else tried either.

"I don't understand this at all," Coach Carlton said. "But if it keeps up, I'm not going to coach you. It's not worth it to me." He turned and walked away, headed for his truck.

Everyone was left standing in the middle of the park. No one seemed to know what to say. Thurlow was already leaving.

Wilson waited a moment, glanced around, and then realized that no one was going to do anything if he didn't. He took off after Thurlow. When he caught up with him, he said, "Thurlow, wait a sec. There's no reason to—"

Thurlow stopped. "Wilson, there's something wrong with you," he said. "Just leave me alone."

"What are you talking about? I just don't want the team to fall apart."

"You can't solve all the problems," Thurlow said. "Gloria is Gloria, and there's nothing you can do about it."

"Okay, fine. But why can't you just forget about her and get out there and play? We could win the championship."

"Oh, yeah. Right."

"We could, Thurlow. We've got some good players."

"Yeah. Like you? You get worse every game."

That hit hard. "Maybe I do," he said, "but at least I'm trying."

"Trying to do what *everyone* tells you. When are you going to start thinking for yourself?"

Wilson had no answer for that. But he had an idea that *was* his problem.

"I don't need this," Thurlow said, and he walked away. This time Wilson let him go.

CHAPTER EIGHT

Wilson tried to think what to do. It took a minute or two before he knew. Then he jogged across the park to his bike. It was a great summer day, but it was getting very hot. By the time Wilson got to his bike, he was really sweating, but he didn't take time to cool off. He hopped on and took off.

He had only been to Coach Carlton's house one time before, but once he found the right street, he remembered exactly where it was and rode straight to it. When he knocked, Coach Carlton showed up at the door, still wearing his funny red pants and a plaid shirt that looked way too hot to be wearing in the summer. "Hello, Wilson," he said. He didn't seem surprised.

Wilson was still breathing hard from his ride, and the sweat was pouring off his face. "Could I talk to you for a minute?" he asked.

"Sure. Come on in."

Wilson followed Coach Carlton into his house. They walked through the living room and on into the kitchen. "Sit down," the coach said. He motioned toward a chair at the kitchen table. Then he took an ice-cube tray out of the freezer. "Are you here to tell me what's going on with our team?" he asked.

"Maybe. I'm not sure I know. But I need to talk to you about me first."

"All right." The coach dropped ice cubes into a couple of glasses, filled them with water from the tap, and then brought them to the table. He sat down across from Wilson.

Wilson took a long drink, and then another, before he said, "Coach, I feel all wrong at the plate. I know you're trying to help me, but I'm getting worse, not better."

Coach Carlton nodded and rubbed his chin. But he didn't say anything.

"Thurlow says I'm listening to too much advice, not doing things my own way, and I think he may have a point." Wilson hoped Coach Carlton wouldn't be mad.

"Wilson, I'm not sure what to tell you. It's true that some good hitters have unusual styles, but I never like to teach a kid to . . ." Coach Carlton's voice trailed off. He must have seen the frustration in Wilson's eyes. "Wilson, listen. When all is said and done, hitting is about two things: seeing the ball and meeting it with your bat. I've got you swinging level, but everything else is all haywire. The plane of your swing is better, but your timing is off—and I'm not sure you're even concentrating on the ball anymore."

"So what should I do?"

"Well . . . I figured, if you were patient, once I had you swinging right, the other parts would come back all right."

"So you want me to just keep trying it that way?"

The coach took a drink and set his glass down. "I don't know," he said. "I don't want you dropping your bat and swinging up on the ball, the way you were. By the time you get to high school, with really fast pitchers, that will never work."

"But, Coach, I feel weird now. Like I'm off balance or something."

"Yeah. I know." The coach took another drink, and Wilson drained off the last of his own water. "I'll tell you what. Maybe you ought to go back to your own stance. It looks funny, but it's what feels natural to you, I guess."

"Yeah. It does."

"But, Wilson, if you drop your bat way down when the pitch is coming, you'll never swing level."

"What if I stand like that, but don't drop the bat so far?"

"Sure. But that's going to take some practice."

"I'll go to the batting cages every day. I'll just keep trying until I get it."

The coach smiled. "Wilson, that's good. But there's something you need to remember. This game is supposed to be fun. If you go up to bat all worried, nothing is going to work. Take it easy."

"I don't want to let the team down, Coach."

"Sure. I know that. But you kids need to lighten up. What was going on out there today?"

"It's hard to say. Gloria makes people mad, for one thing. She tries to tell everybody what to do."

"I know. But she's usually right."

"Maybe, but she makes Thurlow crazy. I'm afraid he's going to knock her head off one of these days."

"Wanda tells me Thurlow's going through some sort of rebellious stage. I guess he's giving her fits."

"Coach, he's not a bad guy. I've known him since we were both little kids. But all of a sudden it's like he's putting on an act—trying to make everyone think he's *bad*."

"Well, kids go through that kind of stuff. I had a couple like that myself."

"Do your kids live around here?"

"Naw. There's no work in a little town like this. I've got a son in Denver, and two daughters in Salt Lake City."

"Are you all alone?"

"Afraid so. My wife died a couple of years ago. We found out she had cancer, and two months later, she was gone."

"You need us, Coach," Wilson said, and he smiled. "We're your kids."

"That's about half right," the coach said, and he smiled too. "But I never did like it when my kids fought with each other. I don't like to be around that kind of stuff."

"I'm trying to work things out—get the players to understand about Thurlow and every-thing—but I don't know how to do it."

"Well, don't worry too much about it. You can't always *tell* people. Sometimes you just have to do things right and hope other people learn from your example."

That made sense to Wilson. His mom had told him he was a leader, and that's what he was trying to be. But maybe he had to find a better way to go about it.

"I'm trying to be patient with Thurlow—mostly for Wanda's sake," Coach Carlton said. "But I'll tell you what. I can't let one kid ruin things for the rest—if that's where the trouble is coming from."

"Don't give up on him yet, Coach. And not on Gloria either. She's trying to do better. And don't give up on the team."

"Well, no. I sure don't want to do that."

Wilson got up from the table. "Thanks, Coach."

"You feel better?"

"Yeah, I do. I'm going to go eat lunch. Then I'm going to head to the batting cages."

"Okay. But remember, probably more than anything, you need to stop worrying so much. Just look for the ball—and try to meet it."

"Okay. That's what I'm going to do."

The Scrappers had an afternoon game on Tuesday, but they had to wait for almost an hour while a thunderstorm cleared out. Most of the players gathered at the Recreation Department building and stood in the front entrance, where they could stay dry. No one was yelling, "Go, Scrappers," but at least Gloria and Tracy were together, so maybe that problem had been settled. And no one else seemed mad.

Thurlow was there, but he was sitting in his mom's car. He looked like a guy waiting for a doctor to give him a shot—with a dull needle.

Wilson told himself he wasn't going to worry about that. He had practiced Monday, and again today, and he thought his swing was coming around a little. He would do his best, and if that meant being a leader, fine, but he wasn't going to try to solve any more problems.

When the storm blew over, it took a little while to get the field ready. The players stretched and warmed up on the wet grass. Wilson didn't know much about the Stingrays, but he had heard they weren't very good. He hoped a win would help pull the team back together again.

The Scrappers were up to bat first, so Jeremy grabbed a bat and headed to the plate. Wanda, in the first base coach's box, shouted, "Let's go, Jeremy!"

The players yelled a little, too, but not with the kind of enthusiasm Wilson wanted to hear. He clapped his hands and yelled, "Everybody hits! Come on, Jeremy, get it started."

But everybody *didn't* hit. In fact, nobody did. Jeremy struck out. Adam hit a weak little roller back to the mound. Then Robbie whiffed on a pitch that sounded like a bomb going off when it hit the catcher's mitt.

When Robbie jogged back to the dugout to get his glove, he announced the bad news to the rest of the team. "I just heard it from the catcher. This pitcher missed the first part of the season.

He was on a trip or something. But he made the all-star team in some league in California last year."

So this wasn't going to be easy after all. Ollie would have to keep the runs down. The Scrappers weren't going to run up a big score, from the looks of things.

At least Ollie looked pretty good when he was warming up.

The first batter for the Stingrays was a guy named Peterson. Everyone called him "Petey." He was a small, redheaded kid who played shortstop. He knocked the dirt from his shoes and looked at Wilson. "Man, those are ugly jerseys," he said.

He didn't seem to be needling Wilson, just telling the truth. "Yeah, I know," Wilson said.

Petey laughed and got into the box. The Stingrays had light blue jerseys with the words *Ray's Tropical Fish Supply* silk-screened on the back. They were probably just as cheap as the Scrappers' uniforms, but at least they weren't the color of decay.

Petey fouled off the first two pitches and

then took a ball, outside. The next pitch came in hard and low. Petey swung and missed. Strike three.

But Wilson hadn't gotten his glove all the way down. The ball slipped under it and rolled between Wilson's legs.

Petey took off for first. Wilson flipped his mask off and spun around, but he couldn't see the ball for a moment. When he did spot it, he got to it quickly, but he knew he didn't have much time. He threw hard but low. Adam stretched for it, and the ball was there in time. But Adam couldn't hang on. The ball dropped to the ground, and Petey went flying by before Adam could pick it up.

Wilson's heart sank. He couldn't believe he had fouled up on the very first batter. Ollie had gotten a strikeout, and Wilson had still put the guy on base.

But Wilson wasn't the only one who messed up in the first inning. The infielders couldn't do anything right. Tracy let a grounder pop out of her glove, and Robbie made a bad throw to second. Gloria might have gotten mad about those plays if she hadn't booted an easy grounder herself.

By the time the Scrappers finally got the third out, they were down 6 to 0, and no one was talking about an easy game.

When that third out finally came, Wilson's mind turned to his other worry. Now he was going to find out whether he could hit this pitcher.

As he searched for the bat he liked, he tried to think of all the things he had been telling himself all week. *Don't drop the bat low. Take a smooth, level swing.*

He watched the pitcher warm up. It was hard to imagine the kid could throw all that fast. He was not that tall, and he was really skinny. As Wilson stepped into the box, the catcher yelled, "All right, Bullet, fire it in here."

"Bullet?" Wilson said.

The catcher was a huge kid. He grinned as he said, "That's what we call him—Bullet Bennett."

Wilson took a deep breath. He tried to put all that out of his mind. *Don't drop your bat too low*, he told himself. *Take a level swing.*

The first pitch came like a bullet all right. And Wilson took a smooth swing. But the ball smacked into the catcher's glove before he was even halfway around.

Start your swing sooner, Wilson told himself. *But keep it smooth. Don't lash at the ball.* He took his stance—the one that felt right to him.

Another fireball! Wilson took a hard swing and—*smack!*—the ball pounded into the catcher's mitt. The big catcher grunted and then laughed. "That one stung," he chided Wilson.

Wilson told himself not to pay attention. He was mad at himself. He knew what he'd done: gone back to his old swing entirely. He had dropped his bat way down and lashed upward at the ball. So he went through his list again, told himself all the things he had to do.

The pitch was low and away. He tried to get his swing started early, then tried to stop it. His weight was thrown forward, and he stumbled, lost his balance, and fell. He ended up flat on his face, his chest across the plate.

And the ump was barking, "Steeeerrriiiike three!"

Wilson jumped up, but the damage was done. The Stingray infielders were all laughing, and someone in the crowd yelled, "Hey, kid, don't hurt yourself."

Wilson stared straight ahead as he walked to the dugout. He grabbed his catcher's gear and started to put it on, but he didn't want any of his teammates to say a word to him.

Robbie did say, "Don't worry about it, Wilson." But Wilson hardly knew how to take that. He'd never been so embarrassed in his entire life.

Wilson was bent over, near the fence, strapping on his shin guards when he heard footsteps coming toward him. He looked up to see his dad coming his way. He really didn't want this.

"Are you okay?" his father asked.

"Yeah. I'm fine."

"Look, I think maybe your problem is that you're not opening your hips. It's just like golf. You've got to—"

"Don't start on me, Dad. I can't think about anything else. I've got enough stuff going around in my head already." Wilson realized his voice had come out a lot louder than he had intended, and now, everyone was looking at him.

But he finished what he had to say. "I'm going to do it my own way. I was hitting fine before everybody started telling me what was wrong with my swing."

CHAPTER NINE

Wilson got into his crouch as the bottom of the second inning began. He signaled to Ollie for a fastball. His mind was still cluttered with all the stuff that had happened, but he whispered to himself, "Forget everything else. Just play your game."

And Ollie helped him out—in a strange way. Wilson could never guess where the next pitch might be, so he had to concentrate.

The first batter took three pitches for balls but then made the mistake of swinging at the next pitch and popping it up for the first out. But that brought up the leadoff batter.

Petey stepped into the batter's box and nodded to Wilson. Maybe he was trying to let Wilson know that he hadn't been one of the Stingrays who had laughed at him when he struck out. It showed some respect—from one player to another—and Wilson appreciated it.

Wilson set up his target outside. But Ollie got the ball out over the center of the plate. Petey caught it solid and sent a hard grounder to the left side.

The ball shot between Gloria and Robbie, but Trent charged hard from left field. He scooped up the ball on the run and threw to second—to hold the runner to a single. But the grass was still wet, and on his follow-through Trent's front foot slipped on the grass. His back leg folded up awkwardly as he hit the ground.

Coach Carlton called a time-out and ran to left field. Trent was on his feet by the time the coach got there, but when he tried to put some weight on the foot, he cringed and then sank to the ground again. Trent's dad hurried down from the bleachers and walked onto the field. All the Scrappers' infielders headed over, too.

"How bad is it?" Wilson heard Mr. Lubak ask.

"I just twisted it a little," Trent said. "It's all right." The coach helped him up again, but Trent stood with all his weight on one foot.

"We better run to the emergency room and have it x-rayed, just to be sure," Mr. Lubak said.

"No, Dad. It's okay. I don't want to leave. I'll sit in the dugout."

Mr. Lubak put his hands on his hips. "Son, that's silly. You're not going to win this game anyway."

Trent had been balancing against the coach, but now he put his injured foot down and stood on it. "What are you talking about? We can still beat these guys."

That was the end of the argument. Trent limped to the dugout. And as he did, Wilson looked at the infielders and said, "You heard what he said. Let's do it!"

All day Wilson had been thinking about his own problems, but it was time to lay off all that and get the job done.

"All right, let's play some D," shouted Gloria, and the Scrappers went back to their positions.

But they had to wait for Thurlow, who was going to play for Trent. He obviously hadn't expected to get into the game so early. He was still lacing up his baseball shoes. But as Thurlow left the dugout, Wilson saw him slap Trent on the shoulder with his glove. It wasn't much, maybe, but for Thurlow, it was something.

Wilson had noticed during the time-out that the Stingrays' coach had had a long chat with the next batter. Wilson was pretty sure they were going to try something.

The way Bullet was pitching, the coach might have figured another run or two would put the game away. Wilson had a feeling that the hit-and-run was on, or maybe a bunt. As he got ready for the pitch, he stayed alert and ready.

Sure enough, the batter squared away and put down a pretty good bunt. But the ball stopped quickly in the wet grass.

Wilson leaped after it. He grabbed it bare-handed and in one motion rifled the ball straight at Ollie, who ducked right on cue. Petey took a headfirst dive toward second. Gloria was off the bag but she caught the ball just off the ground and swung her glove in front of the base in time to make a tag.

Out!

The Scrappers went nuts, and so did all the families in the bleachers. It was easily the best defensive play Wilson had ever made.

Petey stood up, looking toward Wilson. He smiled and pointed his finger, as if to say, "You're the man."

Wilson was psyched, but he felt the excitement, like electricity, run through the whole team.

Ollie's pitching got noticeably better after that. He was finally relaxing and throwing with some natural flow. He struck out the next batter on a red-hot fastball, right at the knees.

Wilson felt the momentum swinging and fully expected his team to get some runs off Bullet. But it didn't happen. The bottom of the Scrappers' lineup came up . . . and went down.

Still, Ollie had found his "zone" now. In the third inning he was still talking to himself, believing what he said, and throwing strikes. He smoked the first two batters and got the third on an easy grounder, ending the inning in a hurry.

The Scrappers' leadoff guys were coming up in the top of the fourth. That was promising, but Wilson knew the truth, too: the Scrappers still didn't have a single hit off Bullet.

But with one swing, Jeremy changed all that.

He didn't connect very well, but he blooped a little fly ball over the second baseman's head for a single.

Now the Scrappers had something to build on, and Wilson felt the confidence all around him. He also saw the first indication that Bullet could get rattled. With Adam at the plate, he seemed to be trying to throw a little too hard. His first two pitches sailed high. And then, when he tried to bring the next one down, he brought it *way* down. Ball three.

Gloria announced, in a voice that could be heard in surrounding states, "There's no gunpowder left in this bullet. Let's get after him."

The other Scrappers took up the chatter. But then Adam clipped a soft little grounder toward third. At first it seemed a sure out, but the third baseman had been playing back. He didn't have a chance unless the ball rolled foul.

It trickled down the line, almost touched the chalk a couple of times, and then came to a stop. Fair ball.

By then Jeremy was standing on second, and Adam was loping into first.

Now the Scrappers were really getting into

it. They hadn't had much to cheer about until now, so they let it all out as Robbie stepped to the plate.

Wilson was on deck. As he worked his way past all the excited players, he noticed that even Thurlow was standing up to watch the action.

Trent was standing up, too, hardly seeming to pay any attention to his twisted ankle. "Come on, Robbie," he yelled. "If you're a star, prove it now."

Wilson stretched out and loosened up, but he didn't take any swings. What he was hoping was that the pitcher was going to pieces; maybe he could work the guy for a walk.

The sky was blue now, but the air was still humid. Wilson took his hat off and wiped the sweat off his forehead. He hoped Bullet was feeling worn down, too. But the guy's first pitch was a rocket. It was close, but the umpire called it a ball.

Bullet charged a few steps toward the plate and yelled, "What are you talking about, ump? That was a strike."

Wilson thought he might be right, but the umpire certainly didn't change his mind, and

Bullet showed his frustration. The next three pitches were *not* close, and Robbie got the walk.

Bullet had been all over the place, but he surely hadn't lost any speed. Wilson didn't think for a minute that this was going to be easy. Even with the bases loaded, he wasn't concerned with being a hero anymore. He just didn't want to do anything to kill this rally.

Wilson watched two balls go by—both just off the outside of the plate. He made up his mind to hold out for a walk. His odds had to be better if he never swung his bat.

But the coach called another time-out. He waved Wilson over and then trotted to meet him halfway. "Wilson, I was just thinking about something," he said.

"I know. Don't swing."

"Oh, no. I don't play the game that way. If the pitch is in there, go after it."

"Yeah, but the way I've been—"

"Listen to me a minute. You've been practicing, working your muscles until they know what to do. But you get in the game and you start thinking too much. Just let all that go. Don't think. Step up there, watch for the ball, and if it's in there, let your muscles do what they know how to do."

Wilson took a long breath. "Well, okay," he said. And he walked back to the plate.

As the pitcher took his sign and went into his windup, Wilson told himself only one thing: *Watch for the ball.* And he saw it all the way. It was right down the . . . *Smack!*

The ball jumped off his bat, a hard line drive down the right field line. Wilson charged from the box, then watched the ball bend into foul territory.

A little air went out of him, but he still felt good. He had really connected; yet he hardly remembered the swing. He had seen the ball, and then the bat had jumped in its way—almost as though he had had nothing to do with it.

Wilson could hear his teammates, Coach Carlton, both his parents—all of them shouting for him. But he put all that out of his mind and focused on the ball.

The next pitch was tough, on the outside edge at the knees. Wilson took a swing and missed. But the swing felt fluid. It wasn't his old swing. It felt better: more level and in control.

But he did miss, and now some of the worries came back. *Maybe I dropped my bat too low again*, he found himself thinking as Bullet went into his windup. He tried to focus on the ball, but he was also thinking, *Smooth swing*, and he watched a perfect strike sail past him. Strike three.

Wilson stared at the ground as he walked back to the dugout. On the way he passed Thurlow coming out of the on-deck circle. Thurlow grabbed Wilson by the arm. "Hey, you've got it back," Thurlow said. "You looked good up there."

Wilson shrugged. "Big deal. I still struck out."

"Hey, don't worry about it. I'm going to hit a grand slam. Then you can come back and make some more Ivan Rodriguez throws to second."

Wilson laughed. He felt a little better.

Trent was still leading the cheers. He was usually kind of quiet, but today he was doing the one thing he could still do. "Come on, Thurlow, whack one out of here!" he hollered.

Wilson saw immediately that Thurlow was serious. He looked the way he did when he batted against the coach. He let an inside pitch go

by, and then he took one on the outside edge
that was close, for a strike. But both times, he
had been set and ready, tempted to swing.

On the next pitch Thurlow took a monstrous
swing—and missed. Wilson could see the relief
in the Stingrays' faces. They knew that if he had
made contact, he would have knocked the ball
into the future.

Wilson also felt the tension around him in
the dugout. Two strikes. If Thurlow struck out,
this rally was almost dead.

Maybe that swing had left something for
Bullet to think about, too. He came with a flash-
ing fastball that hit the dirt and bounced. The
catcher did a good job at stopping it. Now it was
2 and 2, and Bullet wouldn't want to go to a full
count with the bases loaded.

Bullet aimed the next pitch, got it belt high.
Thurlow didn't swing as hard this time, but he
got *all* of it. The ball shot off his bat high and
long, to straightaway center field.

But no one took off after it. The Stingrays'
center fielder just looked up and watched it go.
When it reached the center field fence, it was
still rising. Finally, it landed in the next baseball

diamond, causing quite a surprise for the Whirl-winds and Mustangs, who were in the middle of the fifth inning of their game.

Grand slam!

The Scrappers all piled out of the dugout and met each runner as he scored. They knew they were still down two runs, but they had two outs to go, and it was only the fourth inning. When Thurlow crossed home plate, everyone gave him a huge cheer.

Coach Carlton came down from the third base coach's box to remind the kids that there was still a game going on, but he was smiling, too—big time.

Robbie clapped Thurlow on the back when he got a chance. "Nice shot, man."

Thurlow nodded and smiled. But when Gloria came over to congratulate him and raised her hand high, he looked right past her. Wilson felt bad about that, but he was still too caught up in the excitement to worry much about it.

When the players got back to the dugout, Thurlow walked over and sat down by Wilson. "Well, you did it, Thurlow," Wilson said. "You should call your shot every time."

Thurlow laughed. "Are you kidding? I was just mouthing off. I didn't know if I could get a hit off that guy or not. I was pretty scared."

Wilson hardly knew what to say. He didn't know Thurlow ever got scared about anything. "Well, you came through. That's the important thing."

"Yeah, but I was lucky. That pitcher let up and grooved one for me. If you'd gotten a pitch like that, you would have hit it just as far."

Wilson laughed. "Be careful, Thurlow. You're acting like your old self. You don't want everyone to find out you're not a jerk, do you?"

"Shut up, Wilson," Thurlow said, but he laughed.

CHAPTER TEN

Gloria followed the grand slam with a lightning shot of her own. She knocked a line drive to left center for a double. Then Tracy hit a solid single to right, and Gloria scored. The Scrappers were down by only one, and they were rolling.

And then the luck seemed to turn. Ollie hit a grounder that almost tore the third baseman's glove off, but the kid stayed with it and made a good throw to second for the force. And then Cindy got good wood on the ball but hit a fly ball right to the left fielder.

And that's how things kept going for the next two innings. Even though Bullet was still throwing hard, the Scrappers were timing him, and they were hitting the ball on the nose, getting some hits. But with runners on base, they kept hitting the ball at people. Wilson, on his third at bat, drove the ball hard but right to the short-stop; and Thurlow sent the center fielder to the fence again, but this time the ball stayed in.

To the Stingrays' credit, they were making the plays. And so were the Scrappers. When the game headed into the seventh, the score was still 6 to 5.

The good news was, as the final inning began, the meat of the Scrappers' batting order was coming up. Adam, the number two hitter, was up first, followed by Robbie, which put Wilson up third, with Thurlow to follow—if the Scrappers were still scrapping by then.

But the seventh inning started out like the last couple—with no luck. Adam had hit a hard line drive to the left side, and it looked like a sure base hit, but the shortstop took one step, leaped, and grabbed the ball out of the air.

Adam pulled up and kicked the dirt. All the players in the Scrapper's dugout moaned.

Wilson could only think that he might come up as the Scrappers' last chance. He got his bat and headed out to the on-deck circle. Adam was walking back to the dugout. "Good cut, Adam," Wilson told him. "You got robbed."

Adam nodded. "I think the pitcher has lost a little juice," he said. "We can still get him."

Wilson wanted to believe that.

Robbie fouled off the first pitch, pulling it to left field. That was more evidence that the Scrappers could get around on Bullet now. But Robbie was probably the best line-drive hitter on the team, and Wilson always expected him to do well.

The next pitch was inside, however, and Robbie probably shouldn't have swung. He hit it off his fists and only managed to punch it toward the third baseman.

The guy at third had to know how fast Robbie was. Maybe that's why he hurried his throw. He handled the ball all right, but he threw wide. The first baseman caught it, but he had pulled his foot off the bag.

Safe!

Finally, some luck.

The Scrappers had reason to cheer, and they did. As Wilson walked to the plate, the cheering only got louder. Maybe people were thinking of last week's game against the Hot Rods, when he had hit a seventh-inning homer. But that seemed like a long time ago.

Just look for the ball, Wilson was saying to himself. *Don't try to kill it.*

The first pitch was high, and Wilson let it go.

"Don't try to force it, Bennett," the Stingrays' coach shouted. "Just pop a good one in there. This guy can't hit." The Stingrays' infielders were all yelling the same thing.

Don't listen to any of that, Wilson told himself. *Just watch the ball. It'll be there this time.*

When the baseball left the pitcher's hand, Wilson's eyes were on it. He watched it all the way. It was out over the plate, big as the moon.

When he met the ball, rock solid, a shock wave traveled through Wilson's hands all the way up his arms. But the ball didn't soar high. It shot like a lance, straight over the shortstop's head, into left, and past the running left fielder.

Wilson knew he wasn't fast, but he also knew he was not stopping at first. He rolled around first and charged toward second. At the same time, he saw Robbie pass third and keep going. The throw came in to the shortstop on the cut-off, but the guy had nowhere to throw. Wilson was standing on second, and Robbie had crossed home plate.

It was a great moment. Wilson threw his fists in the air, as much out of relief as happiness. But he was already thinking about making it home with the go-ahead run. "Come on. Bring me in," he yelled to Thurlow.

Bullet was walking around the mound, trying to collect himself. His coach trotted out to the mound. But there was no way Bullet was coming out. He was easily one of the best pitchers in the league. Even if he had lost some of his speed, he was still tough.

Thurlow was probably a little anxious, too. Bullet had been throwing nothing but heat the entire game, and when he used his change-up, Thurlow swung way too soon and fouled the pitch off.

Wilson was surprised the Stingrays didn't walk Thurlow intentionally. He had the feeling they surely wouldn't give him much to hit.

The next pitch was outside, and this time Thurlow reached for it and fouled off another one.

Ahead in the count, now Bullet could really work the corners. But his control was not as sharp as it had been in the early going. He tried to nibble at the outside corner again, and Thurlow reached out and poked the ball. For a moment, it seemed that the ball was heading for right field. But it was a weak little fly ball, and the second baseman ran hard, got to it, and made the catch.

Wilson had come close to taking off. He was glad he had listened to the coach, who had been shouting, "Get back to the base, Wilson."

But now there were two outs. Gloria had to come through.

Wilson loved the look on her face when she dug in. Somehow, as usual, she had gotten dirt all over her uniform, and her short hair was scattered in all directions, sticking out from under her helmet. She looked more like a boxer than a baseball player.

Bullet must have thought he had gotten past the toughest hitter and didn't have to worry anymore. He tossed a good fastball, but it was waist high and over the plate.

Gloria ate it alive. She drove it over the second baseman's head and into right field. Wilson took off like his life depended on it. The coach was swinging his arm in big circles, waving him home.

Wilson hit the bag with his right foot, just the way the coach always taught, and made a straight shot for the plate. With five or six strides to go, he could see the ball arcing down toward the catcher, who had set up in front of the plate.

Wilson considered diving headfirst, trying to get past the catcher's legs. But it was too late. The catcher was sure to make the tag.

Wilson did the only thing he could do. He bolted straight ahead. Just as the catcher made the catch, Wilson crashed into him. Both players went flying, and Wilson ended up sliding across the plate, facedown.

When everything stopped, Wilson rolled over and looked up. A second passed that seemed more like a long afternoon. And then the ump shouted, "Safe!"

Wilson looked at the catcher, who was looking in his glove. But the ball wasn't there. Wilson had knocked it loose.

Wilson jumped up. Finally, he saw the ball lying in the dirt several feet up the baseline. The catcher saw it at the same time and went after it. But by then, Gloria was cruising into third.

"Are you all right?" Wilson asked the catcher.

"Yeah, I'm fine," the big guy said, with no love in his voice.

Wilson trotted back to the dugout, where everyone was celebrating. But the coach was trying to calm them down. "Kids, we've still got to get these guys out in the bottom of the inning. Let's keep our heads now and score some more runs."

The players did calm down, but they didn't get the runs. Tracy got a little too eager and went after a bad pitch. She sent a slow roller to the first baseman, and the inning was over.

When Gloria came running back to the dugout, Wilson saw her slap hands with some of the players and then turn to Thurlow, not realizing who it was. She already had her hand in the air, but then she hesitated. Thurlow slapped her hand this time, without saying anything. When he saw Wilson watching, however, he looked embarrassed. "Hey, Wilson," he said, "nice baserunning. Man, you laid that guy out."

"He was in my way," Wilson said, and he laughed.

"Let's go get this game over with," Thurlow

said, but he spoke softly, as though he didn't want anyone but Wilson to hear him talk that way.

Ollie was riding high on adrenaline, and his first couple of pitches really smoked. The batter finally timed the third pitch, however, and knocked a fly ball into center field. Jeremy held his ground, didn't break, and then dropped back a few steps and made the catch.

"Nice job, Jeremy," Gloria bellowed. "Perfect." The chatter in the infield got louder as the Scrappers saw the win within sight.

But the next batter chopped a high hopper toward first. Adam charged toward it, but the ball took a huge bounce over his head. By the time Tracy got to it, the runner was safe.

There was not much Adam could have done, but Wilson felt his chest tighten. He didn't want to let this game get away after that great comeback. The big catcher was coming up, and he was the one guy on the Stingrays' team who could knock a ball out of sight.

Wilson stepped out in front of the plate and held up one finger. "One away. Take the easy one." He tried to keep his voice calm, to say with his tone, "We're fine. Everything is under control."

But Ollie was nervous now. He was mumbling to himself, wandering around, probably thinking what would happen if this big guy clouted one.

He tried to stay away with his pitches, but he stayed way away, and when he tried a curveball, it broke into the dirt. He walked the batter on four pitches.

Wilson could hear his heart beating in his ears. But he shouted to his players, "One away. Every base is an out. Take the force." And then he looked at Ollie. "You're all right. Just relax and throw the ball to me."

The coach was yelling the same thing.

Maybe Ollie took the idea a little too seriously. He tossed up a pitch that was batting-practice speed. The batter was a sub, who shouldn't have been that much of a problem, but he looped a ball to short left field. It was well over Gloria's head, but it was dropping fast, and Wilson knew Trent would never get to it.

But Trent wasn't out there. Thurlow was.

And he was flying. He flashed toward the infield, dove for the ball, and caught it just above the grass.

In one motion, he rolled over and came up on his feet. And he saw what Wilson had seen. The guy on second had held up, but the big catcher had thought the ball was going to drop. He was halfway to second before he saw his mistake.

Thurlow threw the ball straight as a rope. It got to Adam so fast that the catcher was caught in no-man's-land. Adam stepped on the bag, and that was it.

Double play! The game was over.

For a moment only Thurlow, Gloria, and Wilson seemed to realize that it was over. Wilson ran toward Thurlow, who was grinning and waving his fist in triumph.

Wilson wouldn't settle for slapping hands; he jumped right on top of Thurlow, who crashed to the ground. When someone landed on Wilson, he expected the whole team to pile on, but Thurlow was quick to pull himself loose and get out of the middle of things.

When the mayhem settled down, the Scrappers shook hands with the Stingrays, who were still stunned. Petey even slapped Wilson on the shoulder with his glove and said, "Great game. You guys are good."

"You, too," Wilson said. "We were lucky to win it."

Coach Carlton got everyone together after that, and he told them he was proud of them. "Every now and then, you kids start acting like you're all on the same team. When that happens, we do all right. We're not very good yet. But we could be."

Wanda shouted, "Hey, kids, I've got a lot of cold soda over at my house. Come on over, and bring your parents. We'll have a little celebration."

As people started clearing out, Coach Carlton called Wilson over. He gave him a pat on the back. "You played a good game tonight, Wilson," he said. "Are you starting to feel more comfortable at the plate?"

"I guess," Wilson said. "But I don't think I'm swinging like you wanted me to."

The coach laughed. "Well, you don't have what I'd call a textbook stance, but your muscles are starting to remember what to do. On that hit you got, you met the ball straight on. It was a pretty swing. If you keep batting like that, you'll do fine."

"Wouldn't I hit more homers if I kept swinging the way I was?"

"Not really. As strong as you are, if you keep getting good wood on the ball, you'll hit homers. But you'll bat for a much better average, too."

"I hope so. Thanks, Coach." Wilson was about to turn to leave.

"But that's not the thing I appreciated the most," Coach said. "I like the way you treat people. You know how to stay friends with Thurlow and Gloria at the same time, and no one else can do that. And I like the way you stepped out there in that last inning and calmed everyone down. The catcher has to be the leader on a baseball team, and that's what you're becoming."

Wilson thanked the coach again, and then he trotted to the parking lot, where his parents were waiting. He was a little afraid to face his dad, after the way he had talked to him during the game.

But his dad said, "Great game, son. I was proud of you."

Wilson ducked his head. "Thanks, Dad. I didn't mean to yell at you. It was just that everyone—" Wilson stopped midsentence when he looked at his father. "What're you smiling at?"

"Son, you don't have to apologize. I picked the wrong time to start giving you golf lessons." He laughed at himself. "I just get a little too involved with these games sometimes. If you start playing baseball the way I play golf, you'll be in real trouble."

"It's just that I couldn't concentrate when everyone was trying to tell me what to do. I had too much stuff floating around in my head."

"That's exactly right. And you did the right thing. You used your own head, and you used it well."

His mom was standing a little way off, listening. She walked over. "Way to go, Wil," she said.

"Mom," Wilson said, "the coach just said that I was becoming a leader."

"See? That's what I told you, didn't I?"

Wilson nodded, and then he hugged his mom. When he got in the car, he was still grinning, feeling great, and the funny thing was, he wasn't even thinking about the game.

TIPS FOR PLAYING CATCHER

1. You're the "quarterback" of the defense. You must know the game well. Before every pitch, consider not only the pitch you will call but *all* the circumstances of the game. How many outs are there? Who is on base? What are the runners likely to do?

2. Wear all the required protective equipment. When you're well protected, you feel confident and unafraid. If you're worrying about getting hit by the bat or the ball, you won't play well.

3. Don't worry about getting hit with the bat. Never position yourself way back where you're a poor target for the pitcher. Before you crouch, reach forward with your glove hand. If your hand is six inches to a foot behind the batter's hands, batters won't hit you when they swing.

4. As you give your pitcher the signal, crouch low with your feet close together, your weight on your toes, and your knees spread wide. Hold your mitt in a position to block the vision of the third-base coach. Signal with your hand against your right thigh.

4. After you signal, move into your catching position. Stand up enough to spread your feet wide apart (about as wide as your shoulders). As you crouch, don't spread your knees so wide. Just sit down on an imaginary chair, with your thighs parallel to the ground.

5. Always stay in front of the ball. If the pitch is to the right or left, don't reach for it. Jump out and catch it in front of your chest. This way, you block the ball if you don't catch it.

6. If the pitch is in the dirt, drop to your knees and put the fingers of the mitt on the ground. That way, it can't roll under your glove and between your legs. If the ball is up high, stand up. Don't just reach for it.

7. Think as an infielder the instant the ball is in play. Go out after bunts or slow rollers if you have a chance to make a play on them.

8. On a play at home, get out in front of the plate on the third base line. Catch the ball first, and then look to the runner. Block the plate, get your tag down low, and let the runner slide into you mitt.

9. On a pop-up, take off your mask and find the ball in the air. If it is your catch to make, run to the area, then throw your mask to the side before you catch the ball. If you throw the mask aside before you know where the ball is, you may end up stepping on it. Catch the ball in front of you with the mitt turned up (basket style); that's how a catcher's mitt is designed to work.

10. When the batter hits a ball to one of the infielders, and no one else is on base, run down the first-base line to back up the first baseman. That's a lot of running, but sometimes it can keep a runner at first who might have made it to second.

11. When throwing to a base, come up from your crouch, step in front of the plate, and put your whole body into the throw. Practice hard on your accuracy. Never throw when it's clearly too late. That almost always leads to extra bases for the runner.

SOME RULES FROM COACH CARLTON

HITTING:

Take a balanced stance with your weight slightly more on your back foot (the one closer to the catcher) than on the front foot.

BASE RUNNING:

When you hit the ball, don't drop the bat under your feet, but don't give it a long toss either. Drop it out to your right in one easy, natural motion that won't slow you down as you take your first step from the batter's box.

BEING A TEAM PLAYER:

Don't brag. Let your bat and your glove do the talking. Bragging is not only bad sportsmanship, it can lead to jealousy among players on the same team.

ON DECK:
TRENT LUBAK, LEFT FIELD.
DON'T MISS HIS STORY IN SCRAPPERS #3: *TEAM PLAYER.*

"So what's the deal between you and Robbie?" Wilson asked Trent. "You sound like you're pretty mad at him."

"No. I'm not mad. I just hate all the big talk. And the way he's showboating when he's up to bat. Stuff like that. I'm still his friend. I just hate to see him acting so stupid."

"You gotta admit, though—he's good. And so is Gloria."

"I know that. That doesn't bother me. It's not like I think I'm as good as they are. I just don't want to hear them talking about it all the time."

Wilson nodded.

"A guy should go out there and do his job," Trent said. "If he's good, everyone will see it."

"The worst part is, they may be good, but they make it sound like they're a couple of pros."

"Yeah. Did you hear them yesterday?" In a voice imitating Robbie's, Trent said, "Hey, Gloria, did you see me make that impossible stop, that perfect throw, that . . . blah, blah, blah."

Wilson laughed, and in a booming "Gloria voice" said, "Did you see me catch that grounder with my bare hand—and toss it over my shoulder to second?"

"Oh, yeah?" Trent said, still trying to sound like Robbie. "Well, I dove for one and caught it with my teeth, then spit it all the way to first."

"That's nothing. I'm so fast that I once played shortstop in two games at the same time."

"Well, I'm so good that I played third and short at the same time."

"I played shortstop and center field."

"I played pitcher and catcher."

The two were both laughing hard by then. Wilson's imitation of Gloria was almost perfect. "I played the entire infield," he claimed.

And Trent's imitation of Robbie was just as good. "Puh-lease! I played third while selling hot dogs in the bleachers."

They were both cracking up . . . when they heard a voice behind them.

"You guys are really funny, you know that?"

Trent and Wilson spun around and looked through the bleachers. There was Robbie sitting on his bike.

Trent felt sick.

"If you've got a problem with me, why don't you say it to my face?"

"Robbie," Trent started, but he couldn't think of anything to say. "We were just . . . kidding around."

"You guys just don't have anything to brag about. That's your problem. Every time we get something going, one of you strikes out and ends the inning."

"Hey, come on. Don't start that," Wilson said. "We were just—"

"I thought you guys were my friends. Now I know the truth." Robbie gave a push with his foot and pedaled off on his bike. Wilson and Trent just watched him go.

"Oh, man," Trent whispered. "I can't believe that happened." He bent forward and put his head in his hands.